PAYOFF TIME

"Time for you to pay, Trailsman," Cimarron Sam said, leveling his Colt .45.

"What do you reckon I owe? I disremember owing you much of anything," Skye replied.

"You can think about it whilst you're dying here, Fargo. Seems that I've got a gun, and you don't. So I'll give you a few bullets to remember me by—couple in the legs, smash an arm or two. You can lay here dyin', hard and slow, with flies and other vermin swarmin' round you. Mayhaps then you'll know whether we're even or not."

"Gee, Sam," Skye said, "I ought to make it clear to you that I'm sorry, real sorry."

"Sorry about what, Fargo?"

"Sorry I didn't kill you when I had a chance."

THE TRAILSMAN 88

MEXICAN MASSACRE

by
Jon Sharpe

A SIGNET BOOK

NEW AMERICAN LIBRARY

SIGNET TRADEMARK REG. U.S. PAT. OFF. AND FOREIGN COUNTRIES
REGISTERED TRADEMARK—MARCA REGISTRADA
HECHO EN DRESDEN, TN.

SIGNET, SIGNET CLASSIC, MENTOR, ONYX, PLUME, MERIDIAN
and NAL BOOKS are published by NAL PENGUIN INC.,
1633 Broadway, New York, New York 10019

First Printing, April, 1989

1 2 3 4 5 6 7 8 9

PRINTED IN THE UNITED STATES OF AMERICA

The Trailsman

Beginnings . . . they bend the tree and they mark the man. Skye Fargo was born when he was eighteen. Terror was his midwife, vengeance his first cry. Killing spawned Skye Fargo, ruthless, cold-blooded murder. Out of the acrid smoke of gunpowder still hanging in the air, he rose, cried out a promise never forgotten.

The Trailsman they began to call him, all across the West: searcher, scout, hunter, the man who could see where others only looked, his skills for hire but not his soul, the man who lived each day to the fullest, yet trailed each tomorrow. Skye Fargo, the Trailsman, the seeker who could take the wildness of a land and the wanting of a woman and make them his own.

*Arizona, 1863, not far from Fort Tucson
and the bleak, baking Sonoran Desert.
Here life is measured out in drops
of water . . . and pellets
of hot lead . . .*

1

If there had been a speck of cover on this godforsaken barren chunk of the Sonoran Desert, the Trailsman would have put it to use. He desperately needed to rein up his big pinto stallion, step down, and use his Sharps carbine to discourage the pursuing Apache.

They weren't more than a couple hundred yards behind him. Good range for a rifle, but much too far for accuracy with his long-barreled Colt revolver, especially shooting from the uncertain platform of a galloping horse.

But the only cover within sight was the swirling cloud of dust kicked up by the Ovaro's pounding hooves. Skye Fargo twisted his head. His lake-blue eyes squinted at the Apache, about half a dozen of them. His muscular arm brought the revolver around. His broad shoulders tensed with the ghastly thoughts of what would happen if he should get captured by the Chiricahua Apache. With a deep breath—a considerable task in this swirling hell-baked dust—he forced himself to relax, and took his best shot.

Good. One of the Chiricahua caught it in his bare chest. He slammed back, then tumbled off his sweat-flecked paint pony. His companions reined up a bit as Fargo sent another slug their way. It hit nothing except the ever-present dust, but it came close enough to the lead brave to make him slow the band down even more. The squat chieftain, barely visible through the haze of swirling particles, raised a short battle lance to his side. That must have been a signal to tell the others that it was time to slow down.

Fargo began to turn toward the desert ahead and those blue peaks shimmering in the distance. Given any lead, his well-tended Ovaro would easily outdistance those sorry-looking Indian ponies. Like many tribes, the Apache didn't take good care of their horseflesh. Why bother tending what you have, when it was so easy to steal new mounts as the need arose?

But that wasn't a spear that the band's leader was waving back there. What looked like a short lance was a muzzle-loading Dimick plains rifle with a yard-long barrel.

A half-ounce ball of lead ripped through the Trailsman's right arm. By a hair's width, it missed smashing bones. But it plowed out muscle and sinew in the blood-splashed instant of its passing.

So intense was the shock that the Trailsman saw the exploding cloud of blood and marveled at it for an instant before he felt the impact and suddenly realized that it was indeed his own lifeblood that was spraying outward, then dripping down to the sun-roasted sand below.

He sagged forward and stayed low, the saddle horn pounding at his chest. Riding in a crouch might make those Apache think they'd killed him, and then maybe they'd give up the chase. Besides, it just hurt too damn much to sit up straight.

As the merciful shock wore off, teeth-gritting pain surged up through his shoulder. But Fargo urged his mount on. Still riding at a full gallop, he managed to tug off his bandanna and wrap it around his blood-spurting bicep. Although much farther back than before, almost out of sight, the Apache were still following him. There wasn't any time to stop and bandage his arm properly.

Fargo knew full well that it was insanity for a wounded man to be racing across the desert floor in the heat of day while precious blood oozed from his torn flesh. But even such insanity made more sense than getting taken alive by Apache.

To the rear, the dust plumes kicked up by his pursuers were shrinking, fading into the shimmer and glare of the desert air. Those small Indian ponies weren't keeping up. Fargo gritted his teeth, clasped his knees to his horse, and spurred the Ovaro into one last burst of effort. The Indians were left behind.

The Apache who roamed this outdoor oven between Tucson and Yuma weren't nearly the jockeys that the plains Indians to the east were. So Fargo had eluded them for the time being.

Just how long that might be was guesswork, nothing more. Apache could cover forty miles a day on foot, and double that or better on horseback. They had no qualms about pushing a mount to its death.

In all probability, though, now that Fargo had ridden out of their sight, the Apache would stop to rest their horses, since they wouldn't be inspired by an immediate chase with the victim in sight ahead of them.

But the Trailsman didn't have the option of resting his mount. Foam flecked the muzzle of the big pinto stallion, but he pushed the Ovaro on. The only way they could both avoid getting roasted over Apache fires was to get the hell out of here.

Kicks to the flank weren't having their usual effect on the tired horse. The Trailsman leaned low, so that the horse would catch wind of the blood-soaked kerchief around the top of his arm. Not only was the bandanna dark with blood, his shirt was stiff with it. But even the smell of fresh blood, which generally inspired a horse to hurry to somewhere else, wasn't much inducement. The Ovaro was giving all he had, and that just might not be enough.

Although Fargo was barely managing to cling to consciousness, the irony of his situation struck him anew. He had come so close.

After years of searching for the men who had murdered his parents, he had finally found them. They were out here somewhere. There could be no doubt of that.

A few weeks back, two men had hit an isolated stage station, two hundred miles to the west, over by Yuma. The family there had been butchered and the station burned. That was exactly what had happened to Skye Fargo's family, so many years ago. Afterward, the two men had ridden toward the squalid desert settlement of Persnickety Springs. It was just the sort of sordid place they would feel at home in. Fargo was certain that he had finally caught up to the two men he had vowed to find.

Trouble was, the Apache got to Persnickety Springs before the Trailsman did. Just this morning, he had stopped on a rise, a mile out of town, to eye the isolated settlement before riding in. Nobody was home, except about two dozen looting Apache.

As nearly as Fargo could tell in the moments before he took off himself, the inhabitants of Persnickety Springs had fled with the first word that the Apache were coming. There were many fresh hurried tracks, mostly made by scared people on foot, that led out of town. Unfortunately, before Fargo had gotten himself off the high rise overlooking the settlement, a keen-eyed Apache had detected him.

Now his Ovaro had outrun the pursuing Indians, even though one Apache had gotten lucky enough to tear out a chunk of the upper portion of the Trailsman's right arm. The longer this exhausting, painful pursuit continued, the more likely it was that the Apache would chase the Trailsman, rather than go back to the scene of their looting and then follow the trail left by the departing residents. So Fargo might well be saving the people of Persnickety Springs.

Which was hardly worth the trouble. Persnickety Springs was named for an uncertain water source that sporadically quenched the thirst of about a dozen men who earned their livelihood by hunting Apache. At Fort Tucson, a two-day ride away, an Apache scalp brought a bounty of two to three hundred dollars.

If the men of Persnickety Springs got caught by the Apache, they'd deserve what they had coming. You want to live by hunting Apache, you have to figure the Apache will hunt you. But there were women in the settlement as well as a few children. The Trailsman felt obligated to do what he could to save them.

But he wasn't going to save them. He felt the dizziness engulf him. The heat swelled within him. His lips were parched and cracked. His throat was dry. His horse was spent.

Each stumbling step threatened to land the Ovaro on its knees and hocks. The horse was no longer racing; it was hardly moving. Almost as if he were on a ship at sea, the Trailsman felt the strange sideways roll. But it was hard, gritty earth that met his plunge. He struggled to sit up, but he knew he was never going to climb back up on his horse. There was no reason to. The Ovaro stood splayfooted, head down, tongue lolling.

Mountains shimmered in the distance. Fargo didn't know whether it was because of the heat rising from the valley floor, or because of his own roiling consciousness, but the peaks seemed to float above the ground, drifting on a cloud of lavender.

Fighting to regain his equilibrium, Fargo squeezed his eyes shut. Then, summoning all his strength, he leaned on his good arm and tried to stand up, but he only succeeded in landing flat on his back.

The sky overhead was startlingly bright. He stared into the brilliant heavens, wondering if it would be kinder to shoot his horse. But if there was any time left, no matter how little, Fargo wanted it. He thought the horse might feel the same way.

"Easy there, boy," he rasped, struck by how difficult it was to get the words out.

Pain radiated down from his wounded shoulder and scratched at his dry throat; it clawed at his parched lungs and sat like a weight on his chest, but it was all receding into a curiously numbing ache that wasn't even altogether unpleasant. Fargo closed his eyes. He needed to think, but thoughts didn't come easily. He felt himself slipping away, to a place where the Apache could never reach him.

He forced his eyes open. Black specks swirled in the sky above him. Buzzards, Fargo thought, hoping he was doing the right thing about his horse. "We've come a long ways together," he soothed as best he could with the eerily crackling hiss that emerged instead of his voice. "We've only got a little ways farther to go."

The land sat still and quiet. Only the heat seemed alive—fat, healthy, and wallowing like a pig. But there was life out here—scorpions, poisonous centipedes, Gila monsters, rattlesnakes, Apache, the men of Persnickety Springs, and the men who had murdered his parents. Suddenly it all seemed right. This empty place, so deceitfully beautiful . . . this was hell. Those who lived here deserved it. Fargo was leaving it behind. . . .

At the edge of his blurred vision, the Trailsman caught the shadow of a giant saguaro. Slowly, as slowly as the minutes slipped into hours, the shade crept over him, and the multibranched splendor of the cactus melded into one bizarre specter of gray, its arms outspread like a beckoning prophet. Meanwhile black specks gathered overhead, drifting like ash and blotting out the sky.

From beyond a concealing shelter of thistly desert brush, two pairs of dark eyes watched Fargo.

They saw that the huge black-bearded man lay motionless. He appeared to be harmless, but so did a sunning rattlesnake. The two black-eyed visitors waited cautiously before creeping out from behind their thorny barrier.

One nudged the huge white man with a moccasin-clad foot. The man did not respond. Upon closer inspection, his breath rippled the observer's wild-flowing blue-black locks: the man slept the twilight sleep of near death, but he breathed.

The woman stood up and walked back to her companion. They conferred in an Athapaskan dialect. There were no telltale clouds of dust on the horizon to warn of any approaching Apache, but they would come, for surely they knew of the presence of this white-eyes, and this was, after all, their territory.

The huge bearded man was useless now, but perhaps he would recover. The big black-and-white horse showed hard use, but it still stood. Quickly, because they had much traveling before them, they came to a decision.

The young black-haired woman wore a loose-fitting short gown of trade cloth over her deerskin leggings. She bounded back into the brush, easily avoiding the sharp needles of cholla and prickly pear, and skirting the large clumps of yucca. From the shadows beyond the thirty-foot-tall saguaro she brought out a burro. It had been there all along, hidden in a land that only seemed empty. The donkey's small form was almost hidden beneath long hoselike tubes that in fact were intestines from butchered animals; the tubes carried precious water.

Using their supply of water sparingly, the woman and her friend tended to the Trailsman and his horse before hoisting the huge man over the back of the straining donkey. They headed toward the rocky hills. There they would find *tinajas*, the holes in the rock where the rainwater gathered to give sustenance to the sheep, the bobcats, the foxes, the deer, the Indians and the white-eyes alike. And they would have cover, to shield them from their enemies, who might be anywhere and everywhere.

Dying was not as simple a matter as Fargo had hoped. It seemed that he drifted endlessly, never lighting in one place. His thoughts were filled with dark images, gray perceptions, shadowy snatches.

But surely this was death. His mother was there. He couldn't see her, but he knew that if he could only reach up, he could touch her. His throat ached. He felt her essence, a comforting balm, an impression of murmured endearments.

Or maybe it was all a recounting of earlier events in a life that seemed to be at an end. He'd had diphtheria once as a child, and those days had been much like this. Aware of the dreamlike quality of his perceptions, Fargo tried to shake the fog that befuddled his mind, but the haze would not go away.

He stood on the shoals off the coast of Texas, the flat gray ocean stretching endlessly. But then the waves rose up and rugged crags lifted above the water; it was a gray chill winter's day on the coast of Oregon. The Tetons loomed, heavy with snow, and his snowshoes sank too far into the powdery drifts; he was wet and cold and he still had a long way to go when a grizzly grabbed for him, catching his arm in its fierce claws.

Fargo braced himself as the bear pushed him toward a rocky ledge, but he landed on his back on a street in San Antonio where the glass cut into his arm and the humid heat made him feel sticky and dizzy.

Visions arrived and departed, some of them vague impressions, some dim memories, some vivid jolts that startled him almost to wakefulness. But as the days passed, the only absolute reality Fargo knew was the sweating, the shivering, the pain.

Gradually the pain eased, but the drifting continued. The images melded into something soothing and warm. The discontinuity of his thoughts no longer bothered him; he felt for sure he was in heaven. The voice that crooned to him was closer and more defined. The angel spoke to him in Spanish.

A horse nickered. Fargo opened his eyes and the Ovaro stood nearby. It seemed a marvelous thing that they had arrived at this place together, and he felt better; he was becoming accustomed to this disjointed existence.

Voices came to him, sometimes the one in Spanish and sometimes from farther away a whispered conversation in an Indian dialect. Fargo didn't understand the words. Then he heard a voice in English. It seemed as if he had gone forever since hearing words he could understand, and he strained his ears to listen.

"You give him too much of the white-eyes' medicine," one voice warned.

"*Sí*, but he lives," another replied. Or maybe it wasn't another voice, but just the first one talking to herself. He couldn't be sure.

At first the words meant nothing to him, but slowly he interpreted their message with growing certainty. He was alive. Yet if he was alive, why did he persist in this endless drifting?

No longer content to exist in a world of formless gray, Fargo fought as hard for consciousness as he had ever fought for anything. He knew he tossed and turned, he knew he thrashed and groaned and sometimes even managed to stand on shaky legs. The woman tried to calm him, but he fought her too. She was still indistinct, something he grappled with as if in delir-

16

ium, but she had arms and legs, a voice that yelled at him, weight that held him down, hair that fell in his face.

Several times Fargo even managed to open his eyes. Once, he would have sworn there was a ceiling of long-needled ponderosa boughs overhead. It hadn't made any sense, and it had sent his mind scurrying in another direction, to the Never Summer Range, to the Wind River Mountains, but the ponderosa had seemed clearer, bolder, less shadowy than the ocean or the Tetons.

Now, whenever the fog seemed to lift, the land was full of piñon. They had to be piñon: short, squat, gray, covered with shaggy-looking cones. But Fargo couldn't trust his impressions. He had fallen out on the desert, far from any cool forest land.

Finally, he found wakefulness when the woman was near. He hissed and croaked at her, determined to talk to her. She spun toward him, her blue-black hair flying behind her. But she wasn't a woman at all, she was a fiend. Where her cheeks should have been, there were gaping slashes; instead of a nose, she displayed a scarred black hole.

Fargo squeezed his eyes shut. Eventually it dawned on him that this was a real woman, an Apache woman disfigured for committing adultery. So he wasn't in heaven, after all. He was in an Apache camp.

Not really a camp, he discovered when he tried to lift his arm. He was trapped down, atop a travois. The two lodgepoles formed a litter that was being dragged to hell knows where by a band of Apache whose only possible reason for saving him was the pleasure they would get from torturing him to death.

Now that Fargo had managed to stay more or less awake for an hour, this was all becoming disgustingly clear. Not that he could see that he could do much about it. His head pounded like a stampede, just from the effort of staying awake. Strapped down and looking up, he couldn't see much except some blue sky and floating clouds. He didn't know, had no way to know, how many Indians were walking up ahead.

Every time the travois bounced, the nausea welled

up. His ears ached with a dull roar that sounded like crashing surf. He wanted to close his eyes; maybe that would get rid of the quivering queasiness that kept trying to smother him. But then he'd be in danger of falling back into that churning sleep that offered no rest.

With painful effort, Fargo lifted his head so he could see to the rear. No doubt there were Indians back there, too, but maybe he'd get some idea of what kind of country he was being dragged through.

Grass. Rolling country carpeted with bunchgrass that was just starting its summer fade from green to tan. Grass? Then they weren't in the desert anymore. But where was he? And why?

Wondering about that was enough to keep his mind busy. He slumped his head back. He would lie quiet, not let anyone know he was awake. By sound and scent, he would find out how many Indians had him. He would figure it all out.

But when Fargo woke again, the sun was high in the sky. It seemed to be standing still and the bouncing had stopped. At least a day had passed, or maybe several days, or maybe months or years. He wasn't even sure he was really here at all. Wherever here was.

Maybe he really was up by the Tetons. Or next to the ocean. Or in hell. Just trying to think made his head feel as though it had been split by an ax. Suddenly he didn't care if the Apache would roast his brains out over a low fire when they found out he was awake. Nothing could be worse than his confusion.

"Where in hell am I?" he roared. His voice cracked from disuse, but the sound still thundered right through the middle of his skull. Fargo closed his eyes against the throbbing pain. Darkness rolled over him, faintness threatened to seize him.

"Señor," a voice called, *"señor,* please."

The Trailsman opened his lake-blue eyes cautiously. The muscles of his face felt as if they had dried and splintered. He opened his eyes warily, preparing for the onslaught of sunlight and headache.

The woman leaning over him was pretty and almost

18

definitely Spanish—not Mexican, but Spanish. Her face was thin, her nose was small and straight, her hair and eyes were dark, but her skin was pale; she appeared to be *hidalgo* without a trace of *indio*. Fargo gazed at her in surprise; he'd expected to find an Apache when he finally saw another person.

"Your wound hurts, yes?"

The woman deftly unwrapped his wounded arm. While she stepped away to fetch something clean for a bandage, Fargo lifted his head to get a look at the damage. Sighing, he laid his head back again. Everything seemed to take a lot of effort.

"First, medicine," she announced on her return, holding up a small blue bottle.

The Trailsman grabbed her wrist and brought her hand in front of his face. "Laudanum," he murmured. "How long has it been since I got shot?"

"More than a moon. As you would say . . ." She narrowed her eyes thoughtfully. "Four, maybe five weeks."

He nodded toward the bottle. "How much?"

"As much as you need. We have many bottles that Querechos take from wagon-train raid."

"Great," he mumbled, lying back to close his eyes. From the slight red streaks still mottling his arm, Fargo figured he had suffered not only from exposure and a bullet wound, but also from a dose of blood poisoning. And now he added an overdose of opium-laden laudanum to his mental list of current problems. But at least he could do something about that one.

"I don't want any more," he insisted as she pushed a spoon toward his lips.

"But, *señor*, without medicine you have much pain," she protested.

"So be it," he muttered. Fargo felt the woman start to withdraw. He wasn't in any kind of shape to attempt an escape yet, but he couldn't just let her go.

"Wait," he called, opening his eyes once again. "Where are you taking me?"

The woman came back and stooped down beside him. Her brows furrowed with puzzlement, and Fargo concluded that although she seemed well-versed in English, in all likelihood she seldom spoke it.

"We not take you. You take us."

"Us?" he demanded.

"My sister and I."

"So I'm taking you," he muttered skeptically. "And just where am I supposed to be taking you?"

"Mexico."

"Why aren't you just taking yourselves?" he asked, feeling swamped by confusion and dizziness.

"We not know where it is."

Fargo couldn't help but grin, even though it threatened to shatter every bone in his face. "Where are we now?"

"Over Gila Mountains, in place some call Nuevo Mexico. I think maybe near city of Santa Fe, maybe not." She shrugged.

"You've got to be joshing," he blurted. They were at least three hundred miles from where he had fallen, maybe five hundred. Fargo couldn't believe his luck. Not because he was out of Apache territory—he wasn't. Actually, he was in the heart of that land where Apache, Pueblo, Pima, Comanche, Ute, Kiowa, and Kiowa Apache roamed. He was flat on his back in the most hostile territory on the continent, and yet he was the guide. But at least there were no Chiricahua on his tail.

"How did you know I could find Mexico?" Fargo wondered aloud.

"We not know. We hope. My sister is Apache, so we dare not enter white city to ask way."

Fargo felt like laughing. Later, he'd figure out why this Spanish woman's sister was a disfigured Apache woman, and what he would do about things. Right now, his legs were cramping something terrible, his face itched as if a thousand ants were crawling inside it, and his head still throbbed wildly. Not to mention his arm, which seemed intent on demonstrating new ways to send pain across his back and chest.

Momentarily, Fargo remembered how close he had finally come to getting his two men, and a flash of regret added to his discomfort. Those two had slipped through his fingers time and again, and they had done it once more. They were hundreds of miles away, and it looked as though the Trailsman was bound for Mexico.

But Fargo felt relieved and giddy, nonetheless. For once, a woman's damnable sense of direction had served him well.

2

The Trailsman could think of several hundred things, from overflowing privies to angered skunks, that smelled better than the herb poultice that clung to his wounded shoulder like an epaulet. But he had to concede that the foul-smelling pledget was doing the job. The furrow left in his flesh by that Apache bullet was healing cleanly. It was scabbed over and it did not fester or ooze with infection.

Even so, he wasn't likely to forget about the wound in the near future. Every time he lifted or extended his right arm, pangs assaulted his rib cage, front and back, on that side of his torso. The spasms surged up again as he tugged the broad brim of his hat even lower so that the red ball rising in the east wouldn't glare quite so much.

It was time to get some decent idea of where he was after getting hauled, mostly unconscious, across half the Southwest by two women whose names he didn't know. They were still slumbering in camp, a quarter-mile down slope, near the bottom of a draw. Fargo stood on the rise amid sagebrush and yucca, scanning the countryside.

This time of the summer, the sun would be rising somewhat north of due east. Besides the sun, there wasn't much to notice, anywhere to the east. Just rolling prairie, treeless and barren, dotted with a few buttes. Perhaps twenty miles to the west, mountains reared up.

Shit, he thought. This could be anywhere in the fifteen hundred miles from Canada to Mexico where the Great Plains met the Rockies. But the land looked mighty dry, and the younger woman had said something about thinking they were somewhere near Santa Fe. Not that her sense of direction seemed to be any good, but this did look like the dismal eastern end of New Mexico Territory, fifty or sixty miles east of Santa Fe.

Until he could move around and get his bearings a little better, that would have to do. Besides, it wasn't always all that important to know precisely where you were at any given time. Just as long as you knew how to get from wherever you were to where you wanted to go.

The two women wanted to go to Mexico. Mexico wasn't at all hard to find from anywhere in the West. Just go south. If you somehow missed and got to the ocean first, then you were at the Gulf, and you could just follow the coast westward. No problem there. It wasn't anything that required the Trailsman's skills.

As he started back toward camp, Fargo's keen eyes caught a shimmer rising in the clear air to the west, toward the mountains, which loomed starkly in the low-angled light from the rising sun. He paused and stared intently.

The narrow, rising column that twisted up into the chilly morning air acted like smoke, but it was clear. It didn't obscure the mountains behind it, but it distorted what lay on the other side.

Even if it wasn't smoke, Fargo decided, it indicated a fire not more than four or five miles away. Piñon burned pretty clean, so if you tended the fire carefully, there'd hardly be any smoke. But fires make heat, too, and what he saw was a column of hot air rising from a small campfire. Any later in the day, and he'd never have noticed it, because everything within sight would be shimmering like that one little column, on account of the fierce heat from the pitiless desert sun.

Did that fire mean that somebody was trailing them? More likely, it was just somebody else traveling. But plain old travelers likely wouldn't be so careful about not sending up any telltale smoke.

Then again, why would anybody want to be trailing him and the two women? It wasn't like they were hauling a load of gold. Anyway, the folks back there definitely weren't Chiricahua Apache. If they had been this close, they'd have gone for the kill. Fargo shook his head, but that didn't clarify his thinking worth mention.

All this really meant was that there was something back there to be mindful of. And you had to be mindful all the time anyway in this country if you wanted to stay alive, so it really didn't make all that much difference.

Rubbing his sore arm, he returned to camp. The noseless woman acknowledged his greeting with a grunt, then knelt even lower as she started a fire, up on the bank a few yards away from a tiny twisting eastbound creek that hadn't quite lost its struggle to survive in the desert. Their stock—his Ovaro and their gray burro—stood placidly a ways downstream. He rounded a clump of brush to his bedroll, where he had company: the younger woman.

Actually, she wasn't much more than a girl of seventeen or eighteen. She moved and chattered like a teenager, although her narrow face showed the lines that come from spending a lot of time outdoors. In a loose and dust-streaked calico smock, her damp hair clinging long and dark to her neck and shoulders, she squatted atop his bedroll. Only her dark eyes moved to follow his approach.

"It is time, *señor*, to change the dressing on your hurt." Her English was halting, not at all like the singsong Spanish and rapid-fire Apache that she spoke with her disfigured "sister."

Fargo gritted his teeth and sat next to her. Her fingers deftly untied the cotton wrapping, which she set aside as she removed the mat of rank-smelling leaves.

To keep his mind off how much his arm started to hurt, no matter how gently she probed at the gash, Fargo lifted his eyes from his shoulder to the top of her head. Wet hair meant she'd just washed it, first thing after waking up today. Which meant she'd spent considerable time around the Apache, who thought it was mighty important to wash their hair every morning.

But Fargo had already figured out that much, so his

eyes moved down. If she was wearing anything under that calico smock, it couldn't be much. He had no trouble discerning the swell of her breasts pushing against the cloth with her every motion.

To make sure he'd ignore the pain that assaulted his shoulder, Fargo continued his sight-seeing. Whenever she moved, the loose dress pulled tightly across her chest. Her pert nipples jutted atop her full breasts. As she leaned toward him, her smock gaped loose. Fargo found himself gazing straight down her neck to enjoy the shadowy view of shifting cleavage.

This was almost embarrassing, even though she didn't seem to be paying any mind at all to the probing of his lake-blue eyes. He managed to divert his vision from her exposed breasts, only to note that she was perched so that the hem had risen above her knees, exposing firm and smooth thighs.

The temptation was strong to reach over there with his left hand, just to savor a moment's comfort from touching a woman's soothing flesh. But he thought better of the appealing notion when his eyes moved back up. She was now wielding a short but sharp knife as she trimmed the last of the spines off a prickly-pear cactus pad. His arm started to sting like a wasp bite when she pressed the pad atop the assortment of odd-colored and strange-smelling dried leaves she had already laid into his wound.

So he just sat there, his eyes savoring her, while she finished tying the bandage that held everything in place. Then she stared back at him, her eyes moving slowly from his bearded face down across the sweat-stained and ragged flannel shirt, past his waist along his legs to his boots, and then back to his groin. Just as he had been interested in what delights might lie under her outfit, she now seemed intent on returning the favor.

Not that it would take any real guesswork on her part, since he'd been laid up and she'd been tending him for quite a spell. Besides, he could feel certain stirrings begin to harden; the bulge beneath his button fly was growing more obvious with every deep breath.

She lifted her head. Her glistening eyes met his. "*Señor,* you have other matters you wish for me to tend?"

It sounded like a question, even though she already knew the answer. To demonstrate her knowledge, she rocked back and rose, pulling the knee-length smock over her shoulders and off as she stood.

A surprised Fargo sidled back a bit himself, marveling as she shook her long blue-black hair, which began to billow now that it was dry. All she was wearing was her soft leather moccasins, which had long-fringed leggings that came almost to her knee. She bent over and carefully spread the smock next to Fargo on the bedroll. Then she closed her eyes, swallowed hard, and lay down next to him, her erect nipples quivering as she spread her thighs and arched her pelvis in invitation.

Fargo grudgingly tore his eyes away from her for an instant. Although still early in the morning, they were in broad daylight now. Edgily and hastily, he scanned their surroundings. The campfire, where the older woman had been, was on the other side of some brush. There wasn't another soul in sight.

Even though such quick motions with his reluctant fingers made his tender right arm burn with little jolts of pain, he wasted no time in pulling off his shirt and wriggling out of his trousers.

He rolled atop her, pausing momentarily to enjoy the way her erect nipples tickled at his chest. With no further preliminaries, his yearning shaft found a moist and comfortable haven. With the regular rhythm of a clock pendulum, she rocked upward to get more of him. He was glad to oblige, thrusting down with deep forceful strokes, as if he planned to impale her against the earth beneath them.

Fargo occasionally turned his head and glanced around, although all that was out there was sunshine and cactus. The warm sunshine felt good across his sore back, and the cactus wasn't close enough to be a nuisance. He glanced down at the woman's face.

Her expression hadn't changed since she had invited him aboard. At the rate they were going, a lot of women would have been gasping or giggling or somehow responding. But she just kept her thin lips together in a straight line, not frowning, but not smiling either. Her eyes were still closed. Her arms were not clutched across his back; she had them spread out flat against the bedroll.

Except for the way her middle was heaving up and down, she could have been taking a nap for all that Fargo could tell. But he sure as hell wasn't napping. He pushed ever deeper, reveling in the sensation of flesh meeting flesh.

As his internal pressure built, he wanted to pour himself into her, to somehow submerge into that deep abiding warm comfort that would shield him, protect him from this awful glaring painful external world.

Fargo moved his hands from her shoulders, down her sides, stopping to soothe his palms across the outward curves of her spreading breasts. He moved onward, his fingertips tracing across the sides of her lean and muscled abdomen. He felt his urgency growing, but her steady rhythm continued unchanged, as if she were off in a world of her own, connected to his own by his insistent penetrations.

Even when he slid his hands down to her muscled buttocks and pulled her closer, ever closer, she persisted in her remoteness.

Fargo plunged harder and just quit wondering about her. She was there, and she was enveloping him, and that was all that mattered. With a release that sent shudders from his crown down to his toes, he exploded deep within the strangely silent woman.

His thoughts came back to him. It struck him that she might not have climaxed, that her passions might still be building. He stayed in the saddle, but now she was motionless, as inert and unresponsive as the bedroll beneath her dress. Mindful of his sore shoulder, he rolled off gingerly, caressing her shoulders as he eased away.

Finally she opened her eyes and then her mouth. "You are done now, *señor*? Or do you wish to do more?"

Even the jaded three-ways-for-six-bits whores that you found near an army camp displayed more interest and excitement than she had. Fargo tried to summon an answer. "Guess so," was the best he could do as he looked about for his shirt.

She sat up, sidled over, grabbed her smock, and started pulling it on.

Maybe conversation would improve matters here, he thought as he helped her get her arms through the dress. He started asking questions. "Who are you? Who's your sister? Why do you want to go to Mexico?"

"Who are you? Where were you going?" she replied, her lips still drawn. "All I know is we find you in desert far away and you look big and strong, like maybe someone who could help my sister and me."

"Maybe I could," Fargo conceded. He thought of how his sorely wounded shoulder was healing. "You've helped me, I think. I'm Skye Fargo. Some call me the Trailsman." Although such a greeting seemed kind of foolish after what they'd just been doing, he stuck out his hand to shake.

She grasped it and held it tight. "This person has many names." Her voice wasn't much more than a whisper as her eyes met his. "I was once called Carmina María Dolores Gallegos y Hernández. I have been called Pale Woman, That Woman, Bird Woman—what name I am called by matters not."

Judging by her husky monotone, not much of anything mattered to her. "What do you want me to call you?" Fargo prodded.

"Whatever you wish. It is not for me to say."

The Trailsman finished buttoning his shirt and looked around before standing to pull on his denim trousers. "Then I'll call you Carmina. It's a pretty name, and you're a pretty girl." He smiled, but if she noticed, she didn't let on.

Carmina shrugged, then stood. "As I said, whatever you wish, Señor Fargo."

He stepped over to her side as they began slowly walking around the brush and down the draw toward the campfire. "Then, what I wish, Carmina, is for you to tell me something about yourself and what's going on around here. Who's this woman you call your sister? If you two are blood sisters, then my Ovaro and that burro of yours could be blood brothers."

Over breakfast—fried chunks of rabbit that the

noseless woman had caught in a snare—Carmina explained her situation to the Trailsman.

She had been born, seventeen or eighteen years ago—she'd lost count—in northern Mexico. Not far from Chihuahua, her family home was a once-prosperous hacienda, presided over by her *hidalgo* father, Don Miguel Pedro Gallegos. "It was a big rancho, with many beefs and muttons. Then the Apache began to raid.

"First they just take our herds and flocks," Carmina continued. "Then they move closer. One night four-five years ago, they reach the great house, kill my duenna when she struggled against them, and they carry me off."

"You were just a twelve-year-old girl then," Fargo muttered, his mouth and throat growing dry at the thought of a little girl being hauled away by the Apache.

"But I was growing a woman's body, and that was all that the Mimbreno cared about. I could carry much and tan hides and grind corn like the other women in that band of Apache."

"You've been Apache ever since?" Fargo provoked.

She shook her head. "The Comanche raid, steal me and other women from Mimbreno, along with many horses. Mimbreno respect me, save me for a wife, but not Comanche. They pass me around, take turns on top of me, night after night."

So that's why Carmina wasn't exactly an energetic bed partner. She just figured that it was something men did to you, and you'd best just lie back and cooperate if you didn't want them to turn surly on you.

Carmina interrupted Fargo's sad sigh as she continued. "Somewhere on Llano Estacado, Comanche trade me to Comanchero for guns and whiskey. Comanchero say they want to find my father, get him to buy me back for ransom, but then Jicaralla Apache sneak in on Comanchero and take me. The basket-makers then take me to fair at Taos, where they trade me to the Horse Utes. The mountain people sell me to trapper for keg of whiskey, and Chiricahua steal me from stinking white trapper who never wash hair."

"When was that?"

She shrugged. "A year ago, perhaps. It is difficult to know."

29

"But you're not with the Apache now?"

Carmina pointed to the other woman, who had been sitting there, as impassive as a stone, throughout this conversation in a language that she didn't understand. "Sister and I get very angry with our man, Raven Beak. He spoke not the truth when he accused Sister of sharing bed with other man, but they all believe him and . . ." She finally showed some emotion, gasping a bit as she contemplated Sister's marred face, the gaping hole where there had once been a nose.

But the pause was brief. "He began to say same untruths about me. When men go to raid white-eye village, Sister and I run off with burro. Then we find you."

Fargo gestured toward the silent woman. "Does she have any name besides Sister?"

"That's what all wives of same man call each other."

"That wasn't what I asked," Fargo insisted.

"She hard worker. Always get up early before sun. Meets the day. Some call her Day Woman."

Day Woman? What the hell. It made as much sense as a Cheyenne lady Fargo had once met named Owl Woman.

"Let me see if I've got this straight," Fargo mulled aloud as he turned back to Carmina. "you started out on a Mexican hacienda, which got raided by Mimbreno Apache four or five years ago. You were among the Comanche and Comanchero and a bunch of others before the Chiricahua Apache took you. For the past year, you were a wife there to Raven Beak. One of his other wives was Day Woman."

Carmina nodded as Fargo continued. "And when the braves in your band decided to ride off and raid the settlement of Persnickety Springs, you and Day Woman lit out, hoping to get to Mexico, where you might still have some family to take you in. You weren't too sure which way to go, though. You were just on the run, and then you chanced across me, lying near dead on the desert floor."

"We keep going toward rising sun, where Chiricahua do not go, and take you along and tend you," Carmina finished. "We helped you, now you help us get to my people in Mexico."

Fargo leaned forward and filled himself a cup of coffee before answering. The motion hurt. He wasn't sure he was in any condition for riding a few miles, let alone across four or five hundred miles in the full heat of summer. And if he was where he thought they were, they'd be in for an awful trip across nothing but desert.

"Where do you think Santa Fe is from here?" Fargo asked.

Carmina turned toward the mountains and pointed northwest. That jibed with what Fargo had surmised: they were east of the Sangre de Cristos. If the women had just stopped on the other side of those mountains, back in the valley of the Rio Grande, they'd be right next to the traditional route to Mexico: down the river to El Paso, then along the Camino Real to Chihuahua. But he couldn't blame them for moving on and on and on; they very likely had Apache after them, and that was a considerable inducement to travel fast and hard.

A sun-baked summer trip across the barren thirst-racked plains, down into Mexico, hadn't exactly been in the Trailsman's plans when he'd reined up, what seemed like an aeon ago, on that rise just outside of Persnickety Springs. But it wasn't like he had anywhere else to go right now. Besides, these women had revived him when he'd been close to dead. If they hadn't taken him, either he'd have died down in the Sonoran Desert, or else the Chiricahua Apache would have found him—and then death would have been welcome.

He rose and drained his coffee before turning to Carmina. "Tell her what I am going to tell you." She said something in Apache to Day Woman, who tipped her round, scarred face upward from the fire.

"We have only the burro and my horse. We will need more mounts." He paused while Carmina translated and Day Woman nodded agreeably.

"The white-eyes have a camp not far from here. We will go there to buy horses or mules, then we will go south to your home in Mexico near Chihuahua." If it's still there, which was highly unlikely, he silently added.

About midway through Carmina's translation, Day

31

Woman erupted with a torrent of angry-sounding words that seemed to be aimed at Fargo.

"What's the problem with that?" he wondered.

"She is an Apache, one who has been shamed and humiliated. She says she cannot go near camp of the white-eyes or they will kill her if they do not make her a slave. She adds that you are stupid, even for a white-eyes, because you do not consider such things."

Fargo nodded with the sad realization that Day Woman was dead-right about that. With the wars and raids and tortures and scalp bounties that had inflamed the Southwest, an Apache woman wouldn't stand any chance of just minding her own business if she were around white folks. Just as white folks who just wanted to pass through hereabouts to get to California had a hard time staying peaceable, no matter how much they might want to, if they encountered Apache.

"We'll figure out something so she doesn't have to go into Fort Sumner with me," Fargo consoled.

But Carmina wasn't finished with the translation. "She also says you are not a real man if you would trade gold for horseflesh. You are so far from being a real man that the nose on her face is longer than your male organ. A real man would have enough bravery and cunning to take his horses where he found them. Only a coward who lacked the skills of real men would buy a horse instead of stealing one."

Well, there was another reason why whites and Indians would never get along all that well unless one side or the other underwent a considerable change in attitude. Around a white settlement, a horse thief was a disgusting, loathsome creature that got hanged just about as fast as somebody could tie a knot and find a suitable tree. But in an Indian camp, stealing horses was something to brag on, and a successful horse thief was a renowned hero that all the little kids looked up to.

"Tell her that I have great respect for the ways of her people, but those ways are not the ways of my people. And that if she does not shut her mouth and mind her own business about this, I will trade her instead of gold when I trade for horses. Or I would trade her away, except that she is so lazy, stupid, and foul-tempered that no one would give me anything more than a bucket full of manure for her.''

Carmina gritted her teeth and swallowed hard before passing his message on to Day Woman, whose eyes drew to sharp daggers and she bared her teeth as she spat back her reply. Carmina looked even more upset about translating this.

"She says that you are even more of a coward and less of a man than she thought before. For she is a strong worker and would fetch many good horses in trade. Even so, to trade her for manure would be a good bargain for a wretched worthless man like you. You will soon need a fresh supply of manure to replace that which flows always out of your vicious, unthinking mouth.''

Fargo chuckled. A lot of Indian women liked to pass the time by swapping insults, while they were scraping hides or weaving or grinding corn or tending to whatever other tedious chores women generally got stuck with. Day Woman was damn good with her badinage, even though she and the Trailsman didn't speak one word in common. Traveling with her sure wouldn't be boring, anyway, as long as they could keep it up. Which might be a problem. Judging by the exasperated look on Carmina's lean face, the younger woman was already tired of translating these exchanges.

"Tell Day Woman that even though I am disgusted with myself for allowing the donkey to carry our burdens when she is so much more suited for such a task, I will not take a whip to her worthless hide if she hastens to clean our camp so that we may depart."

Fargo waited for the translation before he concluded. "I have spoken."

3

From the sporadic and tiny plumes of dust, from the occasional tenuous wafts of campfire smoke, from the rising and prickly feeling in the hairs on the back of his neck, Skye Fargo was almost certain that he and the two women were being followed. Had he been feeling better and traveling solo, he would have circled back without letting his pursuer—or pursuers—know what he was up to. But so far, whoever was back there had been keeping his distance and not making any trouble. No sense going out and looking for trouble.

Enough of that probably lay ahead anyway, the Trailsman figured. Fort Sumner was still another day or two away, but it was beginning to look as though their slow progress was a blessing.

Early yesterday, a great cloud of dust had arisen, fifteen or twenty miles to the east. It looked like a buffalo stampede, except there weren't buffalo worth mention hereabouts. The hooves of a Comanche horse herd had raised the cloud yesterday, Fargo determined as they stepped through the churned-up ground.

"If we'd come this way a little sooner, when the Comanche were camped close by, then their scouts might have spotted us." The Trailsman suppressed a shiver at that thought, and continued. "So maybe it's for the best that we haven't been moving quickly."

Fargo had addressed his comments to no one in particular. Which was just as well. Day Woman wouldn't have understood him, and Carmina didn't care.

Just past the next sandy rise, the abandoned Comanche camp appeared.

Tepee rings lined half a mile of draw. From the ridge, Fargo studied the circles of stones that had been used to weight down the tepee covers. Other stones, now blackened, had been assembled into small fire pits. Unused rocks poked up everywhere he looked, in contrast to the sand he'd been traveling through.

The bottom of the draw showed some muddy water, buzzing with insects, where it wasn't shielded by silver-green brush that was a welcome relief from the scraggly creosote bushes, summer-browned bunchgrass, dagger-spiked yucca, and the hundreds of varieties of long-spined cactus.

Although they could have proceeded for another hour or two today, Fargo didn't see how they'd find a better spot to spend the night. Standing beside the Ovaro, he waited for Day Woman and Carmina to catch up, then waved below. Day Woman nodded and led the burro on down.

Carmina halted next to him. "This is where the Comanche were?"

Fargo nodded.

'Their places have bad medicine."

"It's not their place now. They've moved on."

She wrinkled her thin nose. "There is still bad medicine here. I smell it."

Fargo took several deep sniffs. All that wafted up from the draw was the usual scent of where people had been: a mixture of old sweat and privy aroma. He looked over at the Ovaro, whose flared nostrils betrayed his excitement about the scents of desert water and decent forage. If any other odors were perturbing the big pinto stallion, he wasn't letting on.

Carmina glanced at Fargo, then shrugged at his steadfast impassiveness. She shuffled on down toward her "sister," who was unloading the burro as she began to set up camp. He scanned the draw again a few times before following her. After tending to the Ovaro, he climbed the opposite side of the draw.

Back the way they'd come, there was no sign of followers. But that didn't mean anything. Off ahead, toward Fort Sumner, some dust swirled, but it was so far away, and the atmosphere shimmered so much in the heat, that Fargo couldn't be sure whether it was a cloud stirred up by a horse or just a meaningless dust devil.

Something closer, down to his right about thirty yards distant, caught his attention. Half a dozen magpies were convened for a noisy session of pecking and bickering. Mostly because their raucous cries annoyed him as he tried to think on what might be between here and Sumner, Fargo grabbed a convenient rock and heaved it that way.

With a satisfying rustle of black-and-white feathers, the birds scurried off. As nearly as Fargo could tell from his vantage, all the magpie excitement had occurred on account of yet another reddish rock that stuck out of the ground.

But this one was bigger and redder than most, and Fargo couldn't help but be curious as to why the birds had been so interested in it. He was almost there when the rock moved, and he realized he'd been staring at the back of a living man's head, crimson and blistered white from sunburn, maroon and black with congealed blood, streaked by fresh scarlet rivulets where the magpies had been pecking.

This was normally an Apache trick—trussing up a man and then burying him in the dirt with just his head sticking out. But when it came to torture, the Comanche weren't too proud to learn from their sometime enemies. Hoping that the man's face wouldn't be too torn up, Fargo stepped around and knelt.

"Howdy," was all he could think of to say.

As if it took tremendous effort, the sun-reddened eyelids rose. That little bit of motion started trickles of fresh blood amid the close-cropped dark hair. More blood trickled down into his matted charcoal beard. The buried man's gray eyes blinked at Fargo. He moved his cracked lips, barely separating them. All that came out was a hoarse rasp, softer than the rattle of a sidewinder.

A shovel would have been handy, and the man had to be craving a full canteen. But this man had already suffered plenty and would suffer more if Fargo departed, no matter how many promises the Trailsman made about returning shortly.

Like a big dog in a hurry for a bone, Fargo pawed through the sandy ground. Every time a stray cactus spine caught his fingers or a sharp-edged rock nicked his palm, he reminded himself that his pains were nothing compared to what was in front of him.

It was a tedious and sometimes stinking chore, and it might be a waste of time. The man was barely breathing. When Fargo pulled soil away from behind, the man slumped back, as if he no longer had the strength to hold himself up.

His hands had been tied behind him with rawhide, but there, at least, the Comanche had missed a trick. Tie somebody tight with wet rawhide, and the stuff starts to shrink, slowly cutting off circulation as it clamps like a vice. But the Indians must have figured the Apache-style burial was enough suffering to inflict. Perhaps they were saving save some of their stock of cruelty for the next male captive.

Loose sand kept collapsing inward. By the time the Trailsman got below the man's waist and cut the manacles from his wrists, what started as something like a well was beginning to look like a funnel. Now that his hands were free, the man tried to help. There wasn't much he could do, but Fargo told him to start wiggling and worrying himself.

The man nodded, and by working him like a loose tooth, Fargo finally pulled him out of the hole and sliced the bonds on his ankles, just above his bare feet. By resting his flaccid arm on the Trailsman's broad shoulders, and with as much support as Fargo could otherwise muster, the captive could walk.

He sure couldn't talk, though, although all the pieces still seemed to be there. Every time he tried to say anything, he just rasped and rattled. So Fargo tried to deduce what he could from appearances. Although the man's linen shirt and broadcloth trousers were tattered and soiled, they bespoke prosperity. The desiccated man came within an inch of matching Fargo's height of six feet and some, but he lacked the Trailsman's husky shoulders. Even when he'd been eating and drinking regular, he must have been as thin as a fence rail.

They shuffled toward camp, the Ovaro trailing behind. Then the man caught sight of Day Woman. He rasped twice to build up his steam, then let off an ear-shattering howl and tried to twist away from the Trailsman.

Fargo had been around Day Woman for long enough so that her noseless face didn't bother him. But he could understand how it might perturb a stranger, especially one who'd just been an Indian captive. Besides that, it was often the women of the tribe who handled the finer details of torturing captives.

Fargo jerked the thin man around so they were facing each other. "Hear me," he intoned. "We are not your enemies. We are not going to torture you. Fact is, I thought you could use some food and water. Now, sit down and stay sat until I can bring you a canteen. I ain't fixing to hurt you, unless you try to run off. Then I'll do whatever it takes to keep you here with us till you get better. Got that?"

The man nodded and a dust-choked "okay" finally emerged.

From the way the man squirmed when Day Woman went to work on his head, he had good reason to fear that he was getting tortured again. She applied mud poultices to his insect bites and then rubbed an herb that obviously stung viciously to the magpie pecks and sunburn blisters. But after that, and the better part of two canteens, the man was able to talk while the women finished making dinner.

"I thought you were more savages," he apologized, pointing toward Day Woman and Carmina. He eyed the Trailsman. "You have blue eyes and a beard, and you are terribly big for a redskin, but still, with those high cheekbones and the shade of your skin . . ."

"Quarter Cherokee," Fargo explained. "What happened?"

They were in the shadow, now that the sun was starting to slip behind the rise on the west of the draw. But the day's heat still pervaded the area, so it must have been some gruesome recent memory that made the man shiver before he spoke, low and halting. "I came out from the East, looking for a man, and paused at Sumner to inquire. He wasn't there. So I proceeded on west. Two days ago, Comanche scouts caught me and conveyed me to their camp."

Day Woman's excited jabbering interrupted their talk. Carmina passed the message on. "*Señores*, someone is coming, she says."

Must be that cloud of dust he'd noticed to the east earlier today, Fargo decided, wondering how Day Woman, down in a draw, could sense what was happening over the rise, out of her sight. He started to rise, then settled back down, grabbing his Sharps in the process, when he saw the horseman silhouetted atop the ridge, about two hundred yards away.

At the edges of his vision, Fargo checked his own crew. Day Woman and Carmina sat rock-still, next to the fire. They were ten yards or so closer to the creek, still in the sun where the shadow wouldn't reach for a few more minutes. Their newfound companion, whom Fargo had just dug out of the earth, was pressing himself back into it now, right at Fargo's side. He was dirty enough to blend right in.

The high horseman sat atop a dust-streaked bay gelding. It had to be a pretty good horse, since the man wasn't small, and he traveled heavy with twin bulging saddlebags. He wore the usual plainsman's garb. He fiddled with his hat as he continued to scan the draw, much as Fargo had earlier. Aside from the usual rustling sounds as the scant creek oozed from one mud puddle to the next, silence reigned.

Sitting fast with his Sharps before him, Fargo took some deep calming breaths. He could wave and greet the rider and invite him down. But prairie etiquette called for the approaching one to make the first move, to wave or holler or otherwise announce himself and his intentions.

But the man on the ridge was just sitting and looking. Looking into the shady side of the draw where he had trouble adjusting his eyes from the brilliance of the setting sun to the long, brush-choked shadows where the Trailsman sat with his companion.

No, he wasn't just looking. He was leaning forward, slow, as if he were just planning to scratch his horse between the ears. But there was a carbine in a scabbard, and that's what the man put his hand on, slow and easy.

Even that might be understandable prudence, so Fargo sat tight. Waiting was tedious, but it wasn't half as tedious as being buried alive while birds pecked at you and the sun fried you, and the man stretched next to the Trailsman had managed to live through that.

Now the stranger on the ridge raised the rifle. Even that was tolerable. But when the man brought the stock to his shoulder, Fargo figured it was time to match the man's action, even though the horseman wasn't aiming at him. Not at first, anyway. Instead, the muzzle was swinging to Fargo's left, over where the women were perched.

That was contrary to all notions of plains etiquette, to just ride up and start shooting. Time for the man to get an enduring lesson in manners.

The Trailsman's Sharps barked. Fargo was rusty; it had been six or seven weeks since he'd used the carbine. For good reason the gun kicked like a turpentined mule, and his right shoulder was still too tender to put up with much pounding. His shot missed its target, the rider's chest.

But the man's exposed left flank turned red. He rocked back in the saddle, his gun rising so that his planned shot at Day Woman thudded harmlessly into the graveled side of the draw. He tried to pull himself forward, dropping the rifle as he grabbed for the hornless front of his McClellan saddle.

He was almost sitting up straight when he sagged and dropped his reins. The bay decided that was a good time to be somewhere else, and started stepping sideways. In the process, the blood-spurting rider slipped off, down into the bunchgrass and sand. When he lifted his head again, the long-bearded man was staring at the .44-caliber muzzle of the Trailsman's Colt.

"You ain't no redskin," he grunted, trying to reach inconspicuously for the knife at his belt.

Fargo stepped closer, waited for the man's hand to close around its haft, then stomped down hard on his fingers.

The Trailsman lifted his boot and waited for the

spasm of pain to finish crossing the man's creased and scarred face before replying. Now that he saw the twisting red knife scar running back from the man's right eye, almost to his ear, Fargo was sure of the man's identity.

"For once, Cimarron Sam, you're right. Or mostly right. I'm but a quarter redskin. That woman without a nose you were aiming for is likely fullblood. But she's traveling with me, and I don't take it kind when folks just ride up and start shooting."

"I ain't Cimarron Sam," he grunted, sitting up and pressing one greasy hand against the hole in his side, which pumped a little blood with his every breath.

"I has been a spell since I was to a post office and got to see the wanted posters," Fargo conceded. "So I can't say I know what name you're using these days. But you're right. It doesn't matter too much what they call you, Sam. It's what you did that has me riled."

"Who the hell are you? Where'd you come from?"

"From under your goddamn sights, Sam. Man ought to look better when he's shooting. Even if he's shooting at a couple of unarmed women. From what I know of you, Sam, you always were pretty much a shit heel, but I never thought even you would sink that low. You always preferred to abuse womenfolk before you killed them."

"Who the hell are you?" Sam was gritting and grinding his yellow teeth between words while Fargo stood above him.

"Skye Fargo."

"The Trailsman?"

"Been called worse."

Sam collected his breath, and maybe his thoughts. "Our ways never crossed afore. What you got against me?"

"Two men killed in a stage robbery up by Bent's Old Fort last year were friends of mine. Plus there was a muleskinner down hereabouts who was found dead a couple years back. Then a while ago I happened across a hard case you used to ride with, and before he died—died kind of hard, at that—he told me a bit about your murdersome career."

Cimarron Sam got some air in his cheeks, as if he planned to argue, but then sighed and gave up the notion. "Why for you traveling with them redskins, Fargo? Don't you know what's going on here?"

"Just wandered into this country and haven't had time to read any newspapers. So maybe you'd best tell me, Sam. And if I can believe any of it, you just might live."

Sam rubbed his boot-smashed hand against the flesh wound on his side. "Bosque Redondo. Fort Sumner's the headquarters for a big Injun reservation there. That's what's happening here. The idea is to round up all them Navaho and make 'em live there."

"This is quite a spell from Cañon de Chelly, where the Navaho have been living since forever," Fargo mulled aloud.

" 'Bout six hundred miles," Sam added. "But that's what the government is up to these days. Herd all the Navaho out of their slick-rock country to this new reservation, the Bosque Redondo. Not just Navaho, neither. Any redskins we can find—Apache, Comanche, Pima, Ute."

"Trust the goddamn idiots in the government to come up with that one. All those tribes do now is fight, and they've got half the West to roam around in. Their manners aren't likely to improve when they're all jammed together."

Sam nodded, not exactly because he agreed with Fargo. It was obvious that Sam hated to be sitting there in the cactus, wounded and bleeding, while Fargo had a gun out and stood there saying whatever came to mind.

"What the hell are they going to eat there?" Fargo shook his head. "That country over by the Pecos is just like around here—most miserable goddamn land in the world. Hell, there's little game, and even if the Indians were of a mind to farm, they couldn't—not on this land. The government'll promise to feed them— and if any flour shows up, it'll be short weight and crawling with worms. The Indians will just starve. It'd be more kind to shoot them."

"Well, then, you could say I was out bein' kind

today." Sam shifted, just so he'd have an easier time reaching for his revolver if Fargo's attention should waver.

"So you were out taking potshots at any Indians you ran into? And you happened upon those two gals sitting down there?"

"More to it than that, Fargo." Sam sounded almost friendly. "I was out doin' my job."

"Job? You? Paying, honest work?" If sarcasm were negotiable, Fargo would have been wealthy.

Sam nodded. "Got me an honest job, scouting for the army now."

Fargo exhaled between pursed lips. The army had to be pretty hard-up to hire a sometime outlaw and full-time scoundrel like Cimarron Sam, who'd likely been wearing diapers the last time he'd seen an honest dollar.

"I've scouted for the army, and I don't recall it was ever my job to ride up on harmless folks and start shooting."

Sam's head shook from side to side, but his greasy chest-length beard almost stayed put, as if it was holding up his head as it rocked. "Guess you don't know what's going on hereabouts." He went on to explain.

Just this past spring, while passing through Santa Fe, Fargo had turned down a chance to join Kit Carson's expedition against the Navaho, the attack on Cañon de Chelly that was likely going on right now, hundreds of miles away. So the Trailsman knew about that, and he told Cimarron Sam to skip the stuff about how he and Carson were great buddies, which was bullshit, and move up to the here and now.

"Ever hear of General James Carleton, head of the California column that stopped here in New Mexico Territory?"

Fargo nodded. "Name's familiar."

"Carleton got here last year. First he decided to round up the Mescalero Apache to the south and get them inside the Bosque Redondo Reservation. Then he got Carson to go after the Navaho. Now there's standing orders to kill any goddamn redskin that's seen wandering around off the reservation. 'Bout time, too."

"Doubtless there's a bounty in it," Fargo prodded.

Cimarron Sam shook his head in agreement. "Twenty dollar per Injun horse or mule, dollar a sheep, fifty for a scalp."

"And you were so busy looking at those dollars sitting down in the draw that you didn't see me and my Sharps in the shadows," Fargo concluded for him.

"Well, hell, there's recent Comanche sign all over here. Just looked down there, and what was I supposed to think?"

The Trailsman mulled for a moment. "On your feet, Sam."

Cimarron Sam stretched and got on one knee, moving jerkily with feigned clumsiness. If he was going to go for his gun, this was the time he'd do it.

He did. A round from Fargo's Colt tore the long-barreled Remington out of Sam's hand. The fingers that the Trailsman had stomped were now stung, and two were bleeding. Much as Fargo thought the world would be better off if Cimarron Sam no longer walked on it, he resisted the impulse to kill. He had to go to Sumner for horses and supplies there, and his visit would be a hell of a lot more welcome if he didn't kill an army scout, no matter how deserving.

"Jesus, Fargo, you're as good as they say you are," Sam muttered, shaking his hand as a wave of pained shock surged across his disbelieving face.

"Even better," Fargo growled. "How far you figure it is from here to Sumner?"

Sam was looking up, over Fargo's shoulder, as if something was coming from back there. Fargo stepped back and wondered if it was a ruse on Sam's part to get his attention to shift. The man still had one knife on his belt, and his clothes were baggy enough to hide half a dozen other weapons.

With his gun still trained on Sam, Fargo shifted his head. There was something coming—the man he'd dug out of the ground a couple hours ago. He walked slowly, with a gait that indicated that each step was a triumph. A man would feel that way once he got to move after he'd been tied tight and buried.

The Trailsman's attention returned to the army scout. "How far, Sam?"

"Ten miles, maybe. You're damn near within sight of it."

"If you'd been doing your job, Sam, you'd have been scouting out here in time to do somebody some good. Comanche were just here. Left this man behind, just his head sticking out of the ground."

Sam's face drew taut. "Man does what he can, and he can't be everywhere."

"Still, seems to me you owe some, Sam."

"How's that?"

"This man came through Sumner, and you scouts sure as hell didn't warn him that there were Comanche right ahead."

"How the hell was we to know, Skye?"

"It's a scout's job to know," Fargo rejoined. "Why is it that you're so enthusiastic about doing your job when you see a chance for some easy bounty money, but so piss-poor at your work when it means figuring out where the Comanche are? You know, Sam, I don't think that getting a real job has improved your sordid character one whit."

Sam shrugged. "That's as may be."

"Anyway, the way I see it, you owe this man. You're going to head back to Sumner in a couple minutes, but before you depart, you're going to leave him with either your boots or your horse."

Sam looked pained again. "Barefoot or shank's mare across this godforsaken desert, with the Comanche on the prowl?"

"He's got the same choice, Sam. Now, make up your mind while you still have one."

Sam looked at Fargo's Colt aimed between his eyes, ready to blow out his brains. "The boots, then. That bay's good. Won't throw me." He bent, pained by his wound, and pulled off the boots. Fargo helped, and patted the man down to be sure he was disarmed. One boot had a wicked bowie knife. A foot-long Arkansas toothpick was strapped along one arm, under his sleeves. A derringer resided deep in one pocket of his trousers.

Once the barefoot and finally weaponless Cimarron Sam was aboard the bay, he turned. "Skye Fargo, you renegade Injun-lovin' son of a bitch. You'll pay for this."

"Only if you're big enough to collect. Now get your ass back to Fort Sumner, Sam. Or if you're not chickenshit, go earn your pay and follow up on the Comanche that were just here."

As the days' last light played in the vast sky, the army scout headed east at a trot.

But in the other direction, far to the west, a streak of haze rose. From this distance, it didn't look like anything more than smoke drifting off a cigar. Somebody was following them. Fargo was sure of it now, and it was beginning to make him nervous. But not nervous enough to leave two women and a sunbaked man in camp alone while he investigated. It was too risky. The Trailsman stared at the smoke in the distance, knowing he would have to bide his time; he could only hope his pursuers did the same.

Back in camp, he wondered who it was. Why it was. It couldn't be Apache, or more precisely, it couldn't be a band of Apache, for they would have struck by now. It could be the husband of these women. Or maybe it was his two men, and they were turning the tables on him.

4

A little bit of stretching, water, and food worked wonders on the skinny man whom Fargo had dug out. Although the man still showed his age—he had at least a decade on the Trailsman—he didn't look nearly so haggard. He stood easily, and his voice no longer rasped. The Trailsman could even identify a bit of snooty Boston accent.

"Sir, did that ruffian army scout refer to you as Skye Fargo?"

The Trailsman chuckled. "Among other things."

"Let me introduce myself. I am Gideon Caudell Hampton." He extended a hand to shake.

Fargo took him up on the offer, even though it seemed a trifle late for a formal introduction. Then an awkward silence developed.

Fargo got tired of waiting and broke the stillness.

"Okay, so now we know each other's names. That ought to simplify things around camp until we get to Sumner. In case they didn't tell you back in camp, the Apache woman who's missing part of her face seems to go by Day Woman, as much as she goes by any name. It doesn't matter much what you call her. She can't understand you, and she does pretty much whatever she pleases anyway. Most of the time, that's work, so we've managed.

"The other woman speaks some English. She's called Carmina." Fargo pointed to Cimarron Sam's boots, sorely in need of a blacking and lying a few feet away. Then he turned, ready to head back down to camp.

Hampton's bony fingers materialized on the Trailsman's shoulder. "If you are indeed Skye Fargo, the one they call the Trailsman, then I need to talk to you privately."

Fargo looked around. Other than sagebrush, cactus, and a few lizards, they didn't have company worth mention here on the flank of this desert rise. Unless they started shouting, even the women in camp wouldn't hear them. "Now and here will work as well as anything. What's on your mind?"

"When I stopped at Fort Sumner," Hampton explained, "I was looking for a man."

Fargo nodded. "I recollect you mentioned that just before that bounty-hungry asshole showed up with the itchy trigger finger."

"You were that man I was seeking."

The Trailsman's mind raced. Over the years, he'd run across dozens of men who'd made the mistake of trying to kill him. They died instead. But doubtless some of them had kinfolk who yearned for revenge. Obviously cultured and educated, Hampton didn't seem the type to carry on any kind of blood feud—but all sorts of people went west. So it wasn't beyond possibility that Hampton could have had a brother or other kin who had headed for the frontier, taken up some troublesome ways, and had crossed the Trailsman. Even as he thought of this dismal prospect, his hand dropped to the butt of his Colt revolver.

"So?" Fargo finally asked.

"I had instructions to find you and engage you, if possible, in order to perform my mission." Hampton had a long neck, and his Adam's apple scampered up and down its length as he spoke, nervous and hesitating.

"Mission? You a preacher out to convert us heathens?"

Hampton emitted a thin laugh that was about what you'd expect from a man so skinny. "No, not hardly." He was beginning to weave a little, likely because he was getting nervous and he was still weak.

"Then we'll sit down right here and you can tell me about it," Fargo suggested. "Let me fetch you those boots before you run any more cactus into your feet."

Hampton watched with curiosity as Fargo picked up the stovepipe boots, examined the insides thoroughly, then turned them upside down and shook each vigorously. Something about an inch long eventually tumbled out. Fargo pointed to it, then began to answer Hampton's unspoken questions.

"That's a scorpion, and if one gets you, you'll think somebody crawled in and lit a fire under your hide. They like to crawl up into your boots and clothes at night, or just about any old time. In the desert, damn near everything stings, sticks, or stinks. If you're smart, you check everything before you let it near you."

Hampton accepted the boots and eyed the sandy ground below before seating himself and pulling on the boots. "I'm afraid I don't know much at all about traveling anywhere except in cities. That's why I was told to find and engage you."

"For what?"

"You are the Trailsman. You do hire out as a guide, do you not?"

"That is my general line of work," Fargo conceded. "Though lately I can't say I've been doing much of that or any other kind of work. Apache bullet smashed my shoulder a few weeks ago, and I've been more or less laid up." Fargo explained how the women had found him and tended to him, while hauling him several hundred miles during their escape from the Chiricahua Apache band, far to the southwest. "I was feeling halfway able again when I ran across you," he concluded.

"I'm grateful that you did, believe me." Hampton paused and chewed some at his lips. "I guess the place to start is at the beginning. I was an attorney in Boston. Then I accepted a position with the federal government in Washington."

"I sure hope you're not one of the idiots in charge of Indian policy," Fargo interjected.

"No. To put it your way, I work for a different group of idiots. The State Department."

"Foreign relations?"

Hampton nodded. "That's part of it. Here is the situation. How much do you know about Mexico?"

Fargo shrugged. "Not a lot. I've pretty much stayed on this side of the Rio Grande."

"What of Mexico's politics, Fargo?"

Fargo blinked and shook his head. "I don't follow American politics much, let alone some other country's."

"Please bear with me while I explain. The Mexican government, under Benito Juárez, borrowed considerable sums for internal improvements from foreign nations, principally France, Great Britain, and Belgium. Mexico has experienced difficulty in making its payments on schedule. Its government is not wealthy; most of its revenue comes from its customs houses."

"And most of what you pay out at a customs station stays right in the captain's pocket; the government never sees it," Fargo mentioned.

"I have heard of the *mordida* myself, but that is not the issue at hand. There is talk that the French, at least, have landed an army to seize the customs houses. That way, the French can collect the customs income and make sure that the bankers in Paris get their loan repaid."

"I doubt like hell that the Mexicans would just let the French or British or anybody else come in and take over their country," Fargo said.

"Even in Washington, we doubt that too. We know that Britain, France, and Belgium put armies aboard ships and sailed them toward Mexico. And we surmise that Juárez will rally his countrymen to oppose them. But beyond that, nobody up north is certain what's going on. No reliable information comes out of Mexico. My superiors are of the belief that there is a war in progress, and I would be inclined to agree."

Fargo mulled on that for a moment. "Could be. There's talk all over the West that there's fighting down in Mexico. But nobody I've ever talked to seems all that certain about much more. What with Comanche and Apache and Navaho, there's plenty of fighting hereabouts to keep people's attention."

Hampton stretched his bony legs before proceeding. "As far as our government is concerned, the first step is to find out precisely what is happening in Mexico."

"Surprised the government came up with such a sensible notion."

"So I was appointed to leave Washington, make my way across the West, and travel into Mexico to find out what is occurring there. A gentleman in the Interior Department—I would prefer not to mention his name—suggested I find you if possible. He spoke quite highly of some work you did several years ago, guiding one of his survey crews."

Fargo wasn't quite comfortable with that explanation. "What happens after you've found out what's going on? The army is already stretched thin as it is." Fargo's eyes narrowed. "You're not thinking about another invasion."

Hampton stuck out a gaunt hand and steadied himself. "I'm not too sure what would happen. But I know that President Lincoln and Benito Juárez get along pretty well, and that Abe wants Juárez to come out on top when the dust settles. A European army camped right across the border is the last thing that Lincoln or Secretary of State Seward wants to see. They'll do whatever they must to prevent that eventuality. But they do not want to do any more than is necessary, either. There are some delicate issues here, Fargo."

"You mean they don't want it to look like they're meddling with Mexico, but they also want Juárez to throw the invaders out."

Hampton nodded. "That's a fair assessment of our policy."

Fargo stretched his arms. "Hampton, I hope you don't take this personal, but you're about the last person I'd pick for a spy to go into Mexico and find out what's happening."

He laughed. "I shall not attempt to disguise myself. I am an attorney, after all, and I have legitimate business in Mexico. The boundaries of an old Mexican land grant, up north in Colorado Territory, are in contention. My former law firm in Boston represents one party. For all that anyone is supposed to know, I am merely traveling to Chihuahua, the old administrative capital for Mexico's lost northern territories, so that I can examine the archives. Those records ought to shed ample light on the true boundaries of the grant."

That was a mouthful. As the stars began to twinkle

above and the temperature began to plummet from blistering heat to a shiver-producing chill, Fargo formed several questions. "So you want to hire me to get you to Chihuahua?"

"And back, if possible." A sardonic tone had crept into Hampton's voice.

"Well, it seems reasonable. The two women I've ended up with seem to want to go to Chihuahua, too. Fact is, I seem to be the only one around here that doesn't much care one way or another about Chihuahua. I never lost anything there. Anyway, you see any problem traveling with them?"

"Not if I can get accustomed to Day Woman's countenance."

Fargo exhaled slowly. "But there will be problems on account of those women. One is Indian, and the other dresses and acts Apache, even though she isn't. What you just saw with Cimarron Sam was likely just the first round of what promises to be a lot of shooting. Now that the damn government is paying a bounty on Indian scalps, those women might as well be wearing targets. But they tended to me when I was as close to being dead as I ever want to get, so I have a debt to pay."

"As I feel that I owe you," Hampton reminded. "So I take it we have an agreement?"

Fargo nodded, then realized that Hampton couldn't see it by the flickers of the small campfire a furlong distant. "Can you shoot? Can you ride? Just how much of a tenderfoot are you?"

Hampton stood. "I shoot well with a rifle, Fargo. I seldom fall off horses. I simply made the mistake of trusting an orderly at Fort Sumner, who assured me that all the hostiles had been swept out of the territory between there and Fort Union, which was the next place I intended to inquire for you. Since I was attempting to perform my mission with expeditious dispatch, I would not wait until others were bound my way. I rode off alone, which, in retrospect, was a terrible error. A fatal one, in fact, had you not happened along."

Fargo rose as Hampton finished collecting his thoughts and inflicting them on the Trailsman.

"No, Fargo, I have certain talents and abilities. But I am not skilled in the ways of the frontier. If I were, I shouldn't face the necessity of hiring you, would I?"

Fargo laughed and started walking slowly toward the little fire. "I never thought of it that way."

Hampton followed as Fargo continued, grabbing the man when he started to tumble after sending a foot down a rabbit hole. "Okay, we'll get to Sumner sometime tomorrow and see what we can come up with for supplies and stock while we figure out some way to keep those two women from turning into bounty. Then we'll head for Chihuahua."

After a quiet dinner—Fargo wasn't too sure just what Day Woman had trapped to throw into the stew; it could have been snake or lizard—he settled into his bedroll, lightened so that Hampton would have a blanket or too. It wouldn't be all that comfortable for him, but it beat hell out of spending a night in the earth with just your head sticking out. So he doubted that he'd hear any complaints.

What Fargo heard, minutes after settling in, made him certain that Hampton would have no cause for complaint. The faint rustling over in that direction had to be Carmina on her way over to share the government attorney's scant bed. As much as she'd been traded and passed around, Carmina apparently figured it was her duty to service any man that happened to be around.

She was so mechanical about it that Fargo didn't much care whether she visited him at night or not. Carmina displayed about as much feeling as a stone might. Bedding her was better than nothing, but not all that much better.

Then Fargo sensed something near his own bedroll. He decided not to spring up, but lay quiet, opening his eyes slowly. Other than glittering stars against a coal-black firmament, he saw nothing. Even if there were a couple of shooting stars streaking across the heavens, that couldn't have been what he had sensed.

So, whatever it might be was coming in low. It had

happened, a time or two, that a cold-blooded rattle-snake had decided to crawl into a warm bedroll. Couldn't blame the beast, really, but he had different ideas about desirable sleeping partners. Fargo slowly eased his hand over to his revolver. Hitting a snake in the dark would be a chore, but cleaning up after a snakebite was an even bigger chore.

There, to the right. He couldn't see it, but he sensed it. His torso snapped upward. His arm swung down in a lashing arc, for he knew he had a better chance of clubbing the venomous reptile than he did of hitting its tiny head with a bullet.

A starlit streak of rising motion in the overwhelming blackness. The snake was trying to strike first. Its fanged head swept upward, meeting the Trailsman's downswinging arm.

Except it wasn't a snake that caught his forearm. It was a hand. Attached to a woman who let out a soft whoosh of air at the moment of their collision.

She couldn't be Carmina, so she had to be Day Woman. What was she doing, crawling around camp in the dark of night?

Fargo rolled over, bringing up a free hand, and grabbed her arm, silently jerking her atop his bedroll as he rolled back, letting the gun drop from his right hand.

An erect nipple, soft yet firm, grazed across his face as she tumbled across him. All she was wearing, Fargo discovered as his flying hand slid down her back, was a loincloth. She met the strength of his gripping left arm with muscles of her own, twisting her hand so that she could clamp his forearm with surprising force.

Wrestling with near-naked women in the dark may have generally been one of the Trailsman's favorite pastimes. But only when he knew what they were up to, and he had no idea what was going on. He found a pendant breast with his free hand, then moved for the shoulder. He had to get some idea of what she had in that other hand. He suspected that it was a sharp knife with designs on his throat.

She brought up that other hand. There wasn't anything in it except, in an instant, a big chunk of Fargo's upper arm, which she clamped, each strong finger digging into his flesh.

From what Fargo could deduce, he was flat on his back, with only his arms—one of them still hurting—up in front of him, while this silent Apache woman sat astride him, atop the bedroll. She had his left bicep in a viselike grip, while her right hand was twined with his and trying to bend it backward. He could prevent that, of course, with his own strength, but he couldn't figure out what she was after.

Then she started bouncing. Her feet came forward, so she could spring up from them. Still grasping him, she would rise about a foot, then land with surprising force on his abdomen. Her first surprise bounce almost knocked out his wind.

Whatever this was, if it was a game, it was going too far. Somebody could get hurt, and Fargo wasn't entirely sure that he wouldn't be that somebody. But what was he going to do? Tell her, in a language she didn't understand, to simmer down? Ask her politely?

When she rose again for another bruising bounce, Fargo sat up in a flash, snaking himself headward so that she landed this time on his legs rather than his ribs. Applying his arm muscles, he leaned forward, into her, trying to push her back. She responded by twisting and more or less planting a nipple in his mouth.

The succulent flesh came as yet another surprise, but Fargo had never spit one out before, and this wasn't going to be the exception. His tongue explored the little ridges and ravines.

Her hand whose fingers were laced with Fargo's began to move. He resisted momentarily, then decided that he'd let her lead while he maintained the connection. She brushed his fingertips against her flowing hair, then down her side. He felt a scar or two, but mostly smooth, muscled and sweaty skin. Lower, then toward her center, she guided his hand.

The loincloth was no impediment. It was just a belt with a couple of hanging cloth flaps that easily moved out of the way. More hair, not soft, but bristly, pushed at his fingers, and the moistness he felt this time was not sweat.

With strength and urgency, she pressed his hand against her heaving, ripe, spreading center. She rocked against the firmness of his hand, brought a thigh over to increase the pressure, began to gasp in little heaving breaths.

Fargo's knowledge of Apache habits was admittedly sketchy. He actually felt fortunate that he'd never spent enough time around the Apache to learn many of their customs. But as her pulsing pressure against his hand intensified, he felt certain as to what she wanted from him, and his hand wasn't it, even if she had eased her grip a bit so that he could probe her quivering, hot interior with his fingers.

Arapaho women, he recalled, didn't hold with kissing. They liked to nuzzle and rub noses when things were building up. Maybe the Apache thought the same. And if a woman had been sneaking around on her husband, the punishment was to cut off her nose—sort of a way to advertise that if she'd ever been available, she sure as hell wasn't now.

Fargo quit thinking much more about it, though. He rocked forward, pushing Day Woman back. Now it was his turn to be on top, to decide what went where. He paused to tongue her other breast, bringing its nipple up to the same glorious state as its companion.

Her thighs remained clamped about his left hand. They seemed to be locked together, holding his hand in place while she bumped against his palm and encouraged his fingers to probe deeper. From time to time, every five seconds or so, the ring of muscles in there contracted, halting everything except her shudders.

He slid his right hand down, grasping a firm buttock, applying pressure from the rear to match the insistence of his palm atop her. He knew that his throbbing shaft was a better tool than his hard-pressed hand, but she didn't seem to care, and he had no way to tell her. He'd just have to work at it.

Well, it wasn't really work. But he couldn't exactly say he was playing at this, either. A little goose on her rump upset Day Woman just enough so that she momentarily loosed her thigh clamp on his hand. He retracted his fingers in that instant and applied side pressure to one thigh while his bottom hand spread the other.

Now that there was an opening, his shaft found its own way in. A surge of her rising succulence enveloped the throbbing tip, momentarily soothing Fargo's urge to thrust down like a hammer. Day Woman finally said something, from low in her throat. He had no idea what it meant, but the tone seemed to indicate that she was expressing something on the order of "Finally, even this strange and slow-witted white-eyes has determined what Day Woman wants."

But when he pushed harder to give her more of what she seemed to want so much, she slid away, her planted feet and upthrust knees, along with her considerable strength, giving her the leverage to move at will beneath his bulk. The cold night air tore at him; he lunged for warmth and shelter and gained only partial success.

Every thrust was met with a similar parry. If this kept up, they'd be in the cactus and sharp-edged gravel shortly. Maybe that wouldn't bother her, since she'd been creeping through the stuff, but Fargo wanted his knees to stay on the canvas cover of his bedroll.

He quit pushing so hard and let her take control of the rhythm. Her hips rose feverishly, allowing him a slight but delectable gain with each downthrust. Then that band of agitated muscles she held within her clamped down, increasing the pressure and the pleasure. When the tightness continued, he slid back, to come down again and then again.

Fargo felt as though he had to struggle for every fraction of her that he gained. Despite the chill of a desert evening, sweat was pouring off him long before the length of him had begun to plumb her constricting but yearning depths.

Once he got there, Day Woman got even more agitated. She kicked the air, then locked her heels together high above Fargo's pumping back. Her strong fingers pressed against his buttocks, urging him ever deeper while she gyrated beneath him, pressing her open tender flesh against his pubic bone with such enthusiasm that he was sure he'd sport bruises there long before morning.

Her face pressed against his chest, Day Woman muttered as she flicked her tongue across him. She might actually have been making sense, for all he knew or cared. That didn't matter anymore. All that mattered was for him to keep pushing, to immerse himself, to persist until he found relief.

Blessed relief arrived at the same time for both of them, in a glorious internal explosion that ignited her spasming, quivering muscles. As he erupted, she clamped even tighter, trying to squeeze every drop from Fargo, to drain him, to exhaust him.

Beneath the desert sky as some lovesick coyotes sang forlornly in the distance, they stayed locked together. Fargo wanted it that way. He wanted to remain in and on Day Woman for the rest of his born days, never moving. It felt so damn good.

5

Day Woman obviously didn't want to take another step. Less than a mile from the main gate to Fort Sumner, she stood steadfast in the dust, holding the tether of their burdened donkey. Her dark eyes flashed anger that echoed in her disfigured face and the indignant guttural tone of her voice.

Fargo had been several paces ahead, leading the Ovaro while he carried on an idle conversation with Hampton. He handed the attorney the reins and turned to Carmina to tell her to ask Day Woman what the problem was.

"She says she no wants to go closer to Blue Sleeves. They will kill her. Or they will do something even worse and put her in a cage. She says that is no way for real man to treat woman he been under blankets with."

Although they hadn't exactly been under the blankets last night, Fargo could see Day Woman's point. But this walking was getting tedious. No matter how well these women walked, there wasn't any way they'd get to Mexico without horses and supplies.

"Tell her that I will try to stay at her side and yours while we are at Sumner. And that if the Blue Sleeves take her, I will rescue her. I have spoken."

Upon hearing that, Day Woman nodded sullenly and resumed her plodding.

Hampton stepped closer as Fargo began moving toward the gates, walking slowly because hurry seldom paid, and besides, Hampton's feet had to be hurting like hell inside those borrowed boots that didn't fit right. But the man wasn't a whiner. Instead, he had a question. "Do you always travel this way, Fargo?"

"What way?"

The lean lawyer gave Fargo a sly smile. "With women who, well, er, eh . . . ." Normally so full of words, he must have reached the limits of a proper Bostonian's vocabulary when he tried to mention what men and women do together.

Fargo grinned back. "Sometimes it happens that way. A lot of times it doesn't. I don't complain when it does. But you'd best take your blessing when you find them."

"Ah, if you only knew," Hampton sighed. "I was bewidowed a year ago, and in both Boston and Washington, one must be so conscious of appearances."

Even if Carmina barely went through the motions, she would likely seem like manna from heaven to a man who hadn't been with a woman for a year. But there were some things that were a lot better to do than to talk about, and besides, they were fixing to get company any second now as a horse approached, trailing a rooster tail of powdery alkaline dust clear back to the gates of the fort.

His wolfish bearded face shaded by a cavalry trooper's kossuth hat, the sergeant reined up and glared down at them. His sun-reddened countenance softened a bit when he realized that the man in front was Hampton, who'd been through the fort just a few days ago.

"Congratulations, Mr. Hampton." The sergeant smiled. "You've got some considerable bounty coming for rounding up them three redskins here, along with a horse and burro. Who'd a believed that a Yankee lawyer could ride out and round up three of 'em? You want me to herd 'em on over to the reservation while you freshen up and collect your money?"

"No," Hampton thundered, in the imposing voice he generally used for impressing juries. "I want you to get out of our way."

The soldier flinched in surprise, and when his eyes flicked, he saw Fargo's Colt aimed at his forehead.

"What the hell?" he muttered.

"You heard the man," Fargo grunted. "I couldn't have put it better myself. Get the hell out of our way.

We're stopping here to buy some supplies from the post sutler, and to get some horses. Then we're moving on—all four of us."

The sergeant looked yearningly at the carbine by his saddle, but even he had to know it would be pure life-ending foolishness to reach for it. "Mr. Hampton, I don't know what you're up to or why. But there's standing orders that all redskins hereabouts are to be rounded up and put on the Bosque Redondo. Near as I can see, you've got two Indian women, along with a mean-looking breed holding that gun on a soldier of the United States Army."

Hampton seemed ready to talk and Fargo was willing to let him do the talking here. "Sergeant, you'll do us all a big favor if you escort us to your commanding officer, General Carleton."

The soldier looked relieved for a moment, then worried. "Mr. Hampton, the old man rode out yesterday for an inspection up at Camp Anton Chico. Colonel Watson's in charge."

"Then we shall see him. With or without your help, Sergeant."

Trudging through the heat, dust, and flies was even more unpleasant when you were on display. They passed at least two dozen buildings—stables, dispensaries, barracks, bakery, laundry. Every ramshackle frame structure sported windows and a porch, from which stared the curious and hostile eyes of suspicious soldiers, who were getting thirteen dollars a month to go out and kill Indians, and now it looked like three Indians were stepping right through the middle of their fort.

But after an eternity, they got to the headquarters, where an orderly met them on the full-width porch.

Hampton looked ready to kill the pudgy kid with the floury face. "You, Renwick," he barked.

"Sir?"

"You needn't sir me, you pea-brained lout, for I am a civilian. Very nearly a dead civilian, after a slow and painful death while magpies pecked out my eyes, on account of the advice you offered me."

"I'm sure I don't know what you mean, sir."

"I'm certain that you do not wish to know what I mean. Either that, or you lack the wit to comprehend simple English, Renwick. You advised me that there were no hostiles between here and Fort Union. Not ten miles past that gate, a band of Comanche swept through and took me captive."

Renwick reddened and stammered. "But, Mr. Hampton . . ."

"Never mind, Private. Either you were deliberately lying, or else you were speaking of matters beyond your knowledge. In either case, you deserve to be frog-marched, cowhided, and horsewhipped. And then a drumhead court-martial can strip you of that one miserable stripe, hang you by the neck until you are dead, dead, dead—and if the army has any sense after that, they will burn your uniform and pretend that no soldier of your appalling ineptitude ever disgraced . . ."

Fargo rather enjoyed listening to Hampton once the lawyer got up a head of steam. But the performance was interrupted by the emergence, through the door, of Colonel Edwin Watson, who seemed to be in charge.

"What is this?" he barked, with such command and magnitude that even Hampton got quiet.

Nobody answered right away, so the bowlegged and shaggy-bearded cavalry officer looked around to see for himself. After that flitting inspection, he spun on the wolf-face escort. "Goddammit, Sergeant, don't you know that Injuns is supposed to go 'cross the river?"

He turned to the quaking private. "And, Renwick, you likely had that cussin' comin'." His bushy brown eyes flitted to Hampton. "But no soldier needs to take a cussin' from a goddamn civilian. But since you like to run on so much at the mouth, mister, mayhaps you can tell me why you and your breed buddy and your redskin whores seem so intent on disturbin' my afternoon nap."

Since they were right in the middle of a sprawling army post, Fargo resisted his surging temptation to give the colonel a permanent nap.

Watson straightened himself a bit and glared at the lawyer. "I've seen you before, lawyer boy, a few days ago. Mayhaps you can explain to me why for you're back."

Watson's steely gaze would have wilted a lot of men, but Hampton returned one of his own before speaking. "I am requisitioning riding stock, pack stock, travel rations and gear for myself and my guide here, as well as these two women."

"Them squaws ain't goin' nowhere 'cept 'cross the river, providin' they live that long, lawyer boy. You of all folks oughtta know that's the law hereabouts."

"No, Colonel, that isn't the law hereabouts. Both of those women are citizens of the Republic of Mexico who were abducted by Chiricahua Apaches." Fargo marveled at how authoritative Hampton could sound while stretching truth so far.

"Chiricahuas? Got lots of Mescaleros here. But them murdersome Chiricahuas ain't nowhere hereabouts. They range over way across them mountains, far to the south, hunnerds of miles away from here. Lawyer boy, you don't know shit from wild honey."

"They are indeed a considerable distance from their former home, Colonel," the lawyer conceded. "But their original home is in Mexico, and you cannot detain them here, no matter how much you suspect them of aboriginal ancestry. The law is quite clear on that point."

"Law? What law?" Watson stepped back and tried to lean against the plank front of his headquarters building, in such a way that nobody would notice that he was leaning rather than standing soldier-straight.

Hampton cleared his throat. "As you may recall, Colonel, international treaties and the U.S. Constitution you swore a sacred oath to protect form the supreme laws of our land. Among those treaties is the Treaty of Guadalupe Hidalgo, the agreement that ended the Mexican War in 1848."

The colonel coughed. "I follow you so far, Hampton. Now can you get to the point?"

"I shall. That treaty provides that 'In the event of any person or persons, captured within Mexican territory by Indians, being carried into the territory of the United States, the government of the latter engages and binds itself, in the most solemn manner, so soon as it shall know of such captives being within its territory, and shall be able so to do, through the faithful exercise of its influence and power, to rescue them and return them to their country, or deliver them to the agent or representative of the Mexican government.' "

Watson closed his eyes for a few seconds and mulled on that. "In plain English, it says that if Mexicans get hauled off by Indians who tote said Mexicans across the border, then we're supposed to rescue them and return them to Mexico, where they come from."

"That is correct," Hampton added. "These women were abducted from Mexico by savage tribes and carried into our country. So it is your clear duty to assist in returning them to Mexico. Since my business will be taking me there anyway, and I have already engaged a competent guide, I should be glad to escort them."

Watson shook his head. "You may know your law, Hampton. You might even be tellin' the truth 'bout where them flea-bit squaws come from. But you're just some civilian, and this here's a government duty you're talkin' about. So I don't see as it'd be rightful to turn 'em over to you and your half-breed guide here for return. You can just leave 'em here, go on your way, and let me worry about gettin' 'em home."

Fargo interrupted the colonel's humorless laughter. "Just issue us what we need, Colonel, and we'll take care of the rest."

"Can't," Watson grunted. "You two fellers ain't at all official, and besides, you men might well tamper with them squaws. Fact is, I reckon you've already done some tampering, else you wouldn't be so hot to keep 'em."

Fargo tried to swallow the bile rising in his throat, and the presence of Hampton's bony hand on his shoulder didn't stop him from bristling.

"Fargo, could you lend me your knife?" Hampton requested, his voice not much more than a whisper.

If the lawyer wanted to disembowel the rude-mouthed colonel right here, Fargo would be glad to lend him the weapon. He passed his belt knife over.

But Hampton didn't lunge for the officer. Instead, he pulled the pocket of his stained broadcloth trousers inside out. Then he slit along a seam of the exposed pocket and fished out a folded piece of paper. He unfolded it, glanced at it to be sure it was still what he thought it was, and passed it to Fargo while a perplexed Colonel Watson stared.

The Trailsman examined the half-sized sheet of good linen paper. Raised printing at the top said "Executive Mansion. Washington, D.C." Beneath those engraved letters was some spidery handwriting that took a few seconds to read:

> To Whom It May Concern:
> Mr. Gideon Hampton is on a confidential mission of considerable consequence to his country. Please extend to him every courtesy.
>
> A. Lincoln

Fargo whistled. With a broad grin, he passed the note over to the waiting officer. His estimation of Hampton rose. A lot of men would have waved such a note around like a banner as they tried to pull strings and get whatever they needed. Hampton hadn't even mentioned the note until it looked absolutely necessary.

Colonel Watson's face scrunched up, and he took time enough to read the note a dozen times. His receding jaw dropped and got more slack with every reading. Finally he looked up. "Sergeant, get these men whatever they want. Grab an orderly or two and assemble some travel rations, saddles, whatever. Arrange for some rooms in the guest barracks and make sure them squaws get treated civil, or you'll get busted to private and sent to Fort Yuma, you hear?"

The sergeant nodded and scurried off.

Fargo glanced back, and something seemed amiss. He turned further. Carmina was holding the reins of both the Ovaro and the burro. Day Woman was nowhere to be seen. His eyes met Carmina's, and she just lifted her brows in puzzlement, as if to say, "She was here one moment, then vanished, and I know no more of it than you do."

"Did I hear Mr. Hampton call you Fargo, sir?"

Fargo's head snapped back around to the colonel. "Probably," he grunted, his mind on other matters.

Had Day Woman just skulked off to an alley or whatever to answer a call of nature? Or had she decided that the only sensible course, when surrounded by white-eyes and Blue Sleeves, was to lam out when she got a chance—and she'd sure had the chance when everybody had been looking at that little sheet of paper that Hampton was now sticking back in his pocket.

"If you're Skye Fargo, I just received a report from one of my scouts that you shot at and wounded him yesterday evening."

"You'll get more reports like that, and your burial detail is going to get mighty busy, Colonel, if your goddamn scouts keep riding up and shooting at strangers, rather than scouting like they're supposed to. Cimarron Sam somehow missed a whole band of Comanches, but then rode up on us and just opened fire. There may be worse scouts in the army, but I've never run across them."

"Cimarron Sam? The scout that you shot is named Sidney Wentworth."

"Whatever name he wants to use doesn't matter all that much, Colonel. Point is, the man is poor at his work, unless you hired him for thieving and murdering."

"It's hard to get any scouts at all, let alone good ones," Watson snapped back. "But if that man hired on under false pretenses, then he's terminated." With that, the officer spun on the heel of a spit-shined boot and went back inside, presumably to finish his afternoon siesta.

As hot as the sun was, and as tired as he felt after wading through about ten miles of sand this morning, that seemed like a good idea to Fargo, too. The shady porch looked inviting, almost comfortable, especially when a corporal came running over from the stable and led off the Ovaro and the burro.

"Where did Day Woman go? What are we going to do?" Hampton wondered.

"Nothing," Fargo muttered. "Right now, she's the army's worry, so let them look for her. There's lots of men here with nothing better to do."

"But there's that bounty, Fargo, and there are soldiers who might not know of Watson's orders."

"Don't fret. She's Apache. If she can up and vanish from a busy street in broad daylight, it's not likely they'll spot her."

"But how shall we take her with us?"

Fargo couldn't figure out why Hampton seemed to care so much, but then realized that the man was looking ahead to the trip. With two women along, the two men would likely get along better than if there were only one, which made quarrels almost inevitable between the men.

They probably wouldn't admit that they were arguing over a woman who didn't seem to care who or what she slept with. But aggravation and edginess would creep into all their dealings. And when you're traveling in a small party across some godforsaken desert, you don't need any additional aggravation and edginess.

"She'll likely find us when we roll out tomorrow, fully equipped, thanks to that note of yours."

Hampton shrugged. "I suppose that may be so. I hope so, anyway. I owe you an apology, Fargo."

The plank floor of the porch felt softer than feathers as the Trailsman leaned back against the wall and stretched his long legs before him. He pulled his hat down before asking why the lawyer felt apologetic.

"Because I should trust your judgment and expertise on travel matters. You showed confidence enough to trust me to deal with the colonel on a legal matter."

"I had my hand on my Colt, too, Hampton."

The lawyer chuckled as he and Carmina joined Fargo in a siesta. When some late-afternoon stirring roused the Trailsman, he made his rounds, just to see how well the colonel's orders had been obeyed. The sutler and the quartermaster had assembled a decent stock of food and gear, which Fargo signed for. Over at the stables, the remount officer remarked that he didn't have any stock that looked half as good as the Ovaro. In fact, all he really had to spare were five or six big Cordovan riding mules.

"They'll do fine," Fargo granted. "In fact, in desert

country I'd rather have them than horses. They can handle heat and thirst better, and don't eat as much."

The stable supervisor agreed. "That's God's truth, mister. But a lot of gents act too proud to ride muleflesh."

"That's their problem." The Trailsman shrugged. "Like as not, there'll be days I let my pinto trail while I ride one of your mules."

The remount officer nodded at Fargo's good sense and pointed him toward the guest barracks, just across the big corral that held several hundred horses and mules. The animals came in all shapes and sizes, and few were branded. Fargo surmised they represented what the army had so far confiscated from the Navaho and other Indians it was rounding up.

The Trailsman's gear had already been taken over to the guest quarters, a long, low building that buzzed with flies and smelled somewhat rank, thanks to its proximity to the corral. Hampton met him inside, a bit annoyed because Carmina had been quartered on the other end of the long, low building, and there would be an all-night guard in the middle.

"Still no sign of Day Woman, Fargo. Come morning, I suppose we shall have to leave without her."

"Best we tend to ourselves, Hampton." The Trailsman explained his errands and that everything had been assembled for their morning departure. "Think they want us out of here just as soon as they can arrange it," Fargo concluded.

Hampton nodded. "Does look that way, and it is understandable. We've been nothing but trouble for them." He swallowed. "While you were running your errands, I looked after some business, Fargo. Got some new boots and clothing after I cashed a bank draft with the paymaster. And here is an advance on your fee." He pressed a pair of double eagles into the Trailsman's palm.

Fargo shoved the money into his pocket. "Thoughtful of you. Now perhaps I can get us a jug or two."

"Whiskey's damnably expensive here, and of vile quality at that. Perhaps with more cash, we could find some private stock. But all I could arrange for you was standard army guide's pay."

The Trailsman settled down on a cot, his stomach growling for either whiskey or dinner, whichever he could find first. "A dollar a day's better than what a sergeant earns, and I reckon I was headed your way anyway. Let's see what we can do to roust some dinner and then spend some of this on a jug."

The army didn't have regular cooks. Instead, the enlisted men got assigned to kitchen duty, which might explain why they called it "mess" instead of "food." Their meal consisted of sliced beef, fried almost black to the consistency of saddle leather, accompanied by some potatoes boiled to mush, and biscuits that were charcoal on the outside, although the inside was raw dough that could start a stomach churning in nothing flat.

Only the coffee was tolerable. Indeed, it was considerably better than the Taos Lightning Fargo found, although that didn't keep him from enjoying some of the jug, back in the room along with the lawyer. Fargo should have been embarrassed about how he fell right to sleep, even while Hampton was talking.

It was a ruckus outside that brought him to full alertness. He scanned the room, wondering if Day Woman had found a way to slither in here. But except for Hampton lightly snoring on the other cot, it was empty. And besides, the rumbling was outside.

Fargo edged to the window and looked out discretely. The commotion was from the horses pounding around in that big corral. Shaking off the sleep and the liquor, he wondered why he could see those shadowy forms, milling about and rearing to paw at the sky with their front hooves. Then he realized that there was light out there—to his right, toward the stable. Somebody on horseback was waving a torch. No, not a torch. A burning blanket. And the frightened horses were scurrying toward the far end, where a bottleneck of seething confusion had formed while the herd pressed toward an open gate.

Somebody was out there trying to stampede the captured Indian horses out of the corral. The Trailsman quickly realized who that had to be. "Day Woman," he muttered. "Shit."

He grabbed Hampton by the shoulder and shook him roughly, finally rousing him into sitting up. "Gideon, get your clothes on. We're moving out now."

"What, why?"

"Grab Carmina somehow and meet me at the stable fast as you can." With that, Fargo was out the door.

The night guard, a drowsy corporal nodding at a desk in the center part of the barracks, started to his feet as Fargo pounded down the hall. "What's the problem, mister?"

Fargo halted for a moment. "Sliver in my hand. Got up under the fingernail. Hurts like hell. Here, look."

The groggy kid looked down and Fargo's fist came up, knocking him cold and sending him back into his chair. That should simplify fetching Carmina, Fargo reckoned as he legged it out the door. Arriving moments later at the stable, he raced inside and found a coal-oil lantern hanging next to the door. He struck a lucifer and lit it.

The stable's day crew had thoughtfully assembled the pack rigs for the mules, which stood sleeping in the first six stalls on the left, right across from the Ovaro and the burro. The donkey had served them well, but the patient critter was going to have to be left behind this time.

There had to be at least a couple of men on night detail here. Where were they? Fargo cursed the strain on his sore arm as he pulled himself up the vertical wall ladder to the loft and started rousing two sleeping privates.

"Get them mules rigged, soldiers," he barked in the most official tone he could muster. "And move your butts. You goddamn know there's a firing squad for men caught sleeping on duty."

Without waiting, Fargo returned to the main floor. By the time they started down the ladder, he had thrown his saddle and possibles aboard the Ovaro. He led the big pinto out the back door, into the huge corral.

Atop a horse and waving a flaming blanket, Day Woman was halfway across it, pushing the captured horses toward freedom. Since her mind was on her work, Fargo easily got up next to her, although she damn near singed his beard with a furious swing of the fiery blanket.

From the overpowering and disgusting smell, Fargo could tell she had poured coal oil on a sweat-soaked wool saddle blanket. He hollered that it was time to stop this foolishness and get the hell out of there before all sorts of gun-toting Blue Sleeves showed up. But since she didn't understand him, it didn't do much good.

So he grudgingly pulled out his Sharps and swung it like a club. The heavy stock caught the back of her bobbing, angry head. She slumped forward. He reached to pull her to his saddle, but not in time. Her bare-backed pony shifted, and she rolled off on the other side. Getting everything sorted out and rolling Day Woman across the back of his saddle took a few minutes that he didn't know whether he could spare.

By the time Fargo got to the front of the stable, Carmina and Hampton looked as confused and be-draggled as the two rumpled soldiers that were turning the saddled mules over to the lawyer. "Orders said you'd ride out in the morning," one private grumbled. "Thought morning came too damn early in the army anyhow, and this hour's downright ungodly."

Hampton just nodded while Carmina sprang aboard one mule.

"Get aboard, Gideon. We're on our way," Fargo shouted.

The lawyer staggered over to a mule and pulled himself aboard. Fargo reached back to be sure Day Woman was still there, then let the Ovaro rise into a trot after he checked the stars and made sure they were headed south.

6

"Meaning no offense, Fargo, but being as you are the guide on this excursion, do you have any idea where on earth we might be?" Hampton stood in his stirrups and stretched his long frame while his lean face swept the countryside.

He needn't have gone to the trouble. There wasn't much to see. The land rolled a bit, so it wasn't quite as flat as it looked at first. But every direction looked like any other. It was all cactus and creosote bush, dotted with clumps of bunchgrass that was getting browner with every day of unadulterated sunshine and horse-killer heat.

"Sure, I got some ideas," Fargo responded after checking to make sure the two women and three pack mules were still in place. "We're three days south of Sumner, which would come to about a hundred miles, since we've been moving at a fair clip. We crossed the Pecos our first day out. So we're right on the west edge of the Llano Estacado, the Staked Plains."

The lawyer settled back down into his army-issue McClellan saddle atop the riding mule. "Why do they call these the Staked Plains?"

Because the Comanche appear of a sudden, grab tenderfoot greenhorns that ask damn-fool questions, and stake them out atop anthills. That's what Fargo felt like saying. But he swallowed his exasperation along with some trail dust that was so alkaline it made his lips sting.

"To the south there's a line of buttes. They've got edges that from a distance might look like a picket fence, or maybe a line of stakes. That's one story. Another says that those lechuguilla plants that sprout up hereabouts—see that one over there?—look like stakes."

Hampton glanced toward the plant, which wasn't much more than a ten-foot-long stick with a few close-clinging yellow-green leaves near its top. It did look like a wooden stake, and it stuck up about as much as anything did in this vast treeless sweep. The lawyer nodded as Fargo continued.

"Others say that when the Spanish conquistadors first started across here, they found the landscape so monotonous and so easy to get lost in that they had to drive in wooden stakes to mark their way. There are more stories, but the fact is, nobody's real sure why they're called the Staked Plains."

Fargo felt edgy, but decided that it wasn't on account of the lawyer's chattering. He now felt certain that for the past couple days, at least two different parties had been following them.

Judging by the scant sign—a little churned dust, evidence of small fires, tiny whiffs of scents that made the Ovaro and mules flare their nostrils when the wind came from the rear—neither party amounted to more than a man or two, three on the outside. That there was sign at all meant they weren't Indian, or that if they were, they weren't planning to sneak up on the party.

The army was likely more than a little peeved about the ruckus at Fort Sumner when Day Woman had stampeded the herd of captured horses. The most Fargo could get her to explain was that she hated to see any creatures, human or horse, get stuck in cages. Anyway, it was the lawyer's view that since they were traveling on about the highest authority possible short of a divine commandment, the army wasn't about to cause them any trouble. Fargo estimated that the soldiers already had their hands full, trying to keep the Apache and the Navaho from straying off the Bosque Redondo. It would represent a considerable change in attitude for any of those sleepy-heads back there to start looking for extra work.

But somebody was sure as hell back there. Two sets of somebodies. Backtracking to find them, whoever

73

they were, would take time that Fargo didn't want to waste. At least one day for the closer party, which seemed to be about ten miles back, tending to the east. Make it two days for the other one, farther back and on the west, holding close to the Pecos River.

Although the traveling would be easier right along the river, or just over it where there were a few settlements along the west bank, Fargo had veered east. He wanted to avoid people. With this damn bounty hunt going on for Indians, and him traveling with one, it just made sense. Otherwise he'd have to shoot his way through every mud-housed town and flea-bit rancho.

"Isn't the shortest route to Chihuahua through El Paso?" Hampton's question interrupted Fargo's thoughts, but he didn't mind all that much this time, since the thoughts hadn't been all that pleasant.

Fargo nodded. "See you looked at a map before you started your trip. But El Paso's on the Rio Grande, which is on the other side of some mountains that are so far away you can't even see them from here. Besides, they're about as rough as shattered glass, and as dry as a Baptist wedding. If we trend south, more or less along the Pecos, we can skirt the mountains. Down in Texas, where the Pecos swings east, we keeping going south, and we'll get to Presidio."

The Trailsman expected another fool question, but Hampton closed his eyes for a bit, as if he were consulting a mental picture. "That would be right across the Rio Grande from Ojinaga. As I recollect, there is a road to Chihuahua from there. Are you familiar with it?"

"I've heard some tales about it," Fargo confessed. "But I've never crossed it. Back during the gold rush in '49, there were folks that took that route to California instead of the regular trails to the north."

"There as elsewhere along the road to El Dorado, the gold-seekers suffered from great epidemics of cholera," Hampton noted.

Before the attorney could get started on a lecture, Fargo reined up as they topped a gentle rise. A few miles ahead, a cloud seemed to be rising from the prairie. It was as if this land, so heated by the sun, had finally started to boil and give off steam. Except the cloud couldn't have resulted from moisture, not here.

Although it was hazy, on further inspection it didn't look that much like a cloud. It was too dark. It resembled a long bluff, but it hadn't been there a few minutes ago. A lot of strange things happened on the Staked Plains, but bluffs didn't just pop out of the prairie.

Hampton caught the apprehension in the Trailsman's face and came to a silent halt, joining him in staring south. So did the women when they caught up, moments later.

The cloud had popped up so suddenly that Fargo first thought it might be a buffalo stampede. By this time of summer, though, most of the bison would have migrated north, where it was cooler and the grass grew greener.

But it sure did look like a stampede, or at least a moving herd of something that wore hooves. Maybe it was the horse herd from the Comanche band that had taken Hampton a few days ago. But whatever it was, it was coming their way as the morning breeze vanished and the still heat of day took over.

The Trailsman stared at the ears, nostrils, and muzzles of his own Ovaro and the nearby mules. It was obvious they sensed something amiss. The mules' long black-brown ears stood erect and straining, veins prominent amid tufts of short hair. Their flaring nostrils narrowed to slits even as Fargo watched. Beneath the custom saddle, the big pinto stallion was tense and edgy, as if he desperately wanted to be somewhere else. But that was all the animals could tell him.

Fargo rolled out of his saddle and stepped a few paces away from the mules. He flattened himself in the first spot where he wouldn't disturb any barrel cactus. He stretched prone, pressing his ear to the ground. If there was a stampede, the thunder of the hooves would be rumbling in the earth. But all Fargo noticed was giant red ants that seemed hungry enough to gnaw off his earlobe.

Brushing them, along with whitish dust, off his ear, the Trailsman stood.

"Best we find some cover. Pronto." He leapt back aboard the Ovaro and cut west, toward the Pecos, and had galloped a quarter-mile before turning to make sure the others were following.

If they could get to one of those deep, steep-walled draws that dropped into the river valley, they just might live through this. But it was going to be a race between them and the approaching wind, a low and vicious desert wind that was scouring the barren terrain. It was a sandstorm that could bury entire cities, choke horses as they stood, rip the clothes off men and scourge their exposed skin, and convert the silent light of day into a howling hellish blackness of such dark intensity that even the sun would be blotted out.

The broken land next to the cottonwood-lined muddy river was in sight when the first sharp grains of wind-blown sand attacked. Fargo tugged his hat tighter, wrestling with the surging atmosphere for control of the wide brim. His eyes stung and a rasp began to file away at his lips.

He jerked the bandanna out of his hip pocket, holding tight lest the precious piece of cloth get carried north to Colorado, or maybe even Montana. It was touch and go.

Staying aboard the Ovaro was enough trouble, for his mount had been breathing hard with their race to shelter. Now every breath brought choking grit, and the pinto couldn't get his wind.

Sides heaving, the horse stumbled but continued his effort to ignore the reins and head straight into the wind. Horses' hair sloped back from their heads, so they felt more comfortable if they went directly upwind. That might be fine for blizzards, but it could be deadly in a sandstorm.

Besides contending with his suddenly troubled mount, Fargo had to get his bandanna tied around his face, over his nose and mouth, if he was going to have any hope of breathing. His eyes were mere slits when he dared force them open. In the dimness, he used his left hand to hold hard on the reins while sparing a thumb and finger to help his right hand figure out some kind of knot. It would have to be a good knot, because the wind was so strong that its pressure threatened to roll him off the saddle, no matter how firmly he hooked his knees into its skirts.

Finally it was in place, and they were still moving. The deep draw couldn't be more than a hundred yards. But where were the others?

Fargo risked a glance to his rear—a swirling dark ocean of flying sand. It was as if a blanket had been pulled across the once-bright sky. The wind screamed across the prairie. The grains it carried rubbed against one another, adding a low mournful moan to the overpowering sound. Fargo tried shouting and knew even before the dust found his mouth that his sounds would be ripped away before they did any good.

With a stinging and nettled hand, he brought out his revolver. He fired it toward where the sun used to be. The gun was only an arm's length away, and yet he could barely hear its report above the banshee wail of this ripping black roller.

The Trailsman got his gun back in the holster, knowing it wouldn't be good for much until he got a chance to clean it. Windblown grit like this would force its way into every crevice, jamming the hammer and perhaps even plugging the barrel. He stuck his raw-scraped hand up under his shirt.

"Shit," he muttered into his bandanna. Here he was responsible for three people and six mules, and he didn't have the vaguest notion where any of them might be. The women, having lived outdoors in various deserts, might manage. They'd likely seen this before. But they would probably be having trouble anyway, because their mules would be trying to carry them straight into the grinding teeth of this hungry storm.

As for Gideon Hampton, no matter how big a windbag he was, he sure was no match for this. That isn't quite fair, Fargo told himself as he jerked the reins and kicked the Ovaro's flanks, forcing the staggering horse toward the draw that had to be up there somewhere—if either of them still had any sense of direction in this vast roiling abrasive darkness.

It wasn't quite fair because even if Hampton talked

more than any man ought, the skinny man wasn't one of the complainers that Fargo despised. He might not have been precisely the right man for this job of spying out northern Mexico, but it was his job, and he was trying his damnedest to do it. A lot of men that looked tougher than Hampton would never have survived the Comanche burial—or if they had been rescued in time, they'd have turned tail and headed home pronto.

The Ovaro faltered again. Fargo kicked some more, then realized that his horse was stumbling because they had finally reached a draw. Or at least some sort of depression, where they might be able to get down out of the wind.

The Trailsman swung out of the saddle. His shirt came untucked just enough for the wind to catch it. For a moment, it inflated like a balloon. Then the gale caught the back tail and ripped it out of his trousers, snapping it like a whip against the Ovaro's flanks.

Likely the pinto didn't notice, since the sharp-sided grains of sand were also pelting its hide with such ferocity that nothing less than a bullet would get attention. Fargo could almost feel layers of his own skin getting stripped off, as though he were an onion being peeled, as he struggled to put his shirt back where it belonged.

With the wind invading his ears and the sand assaulting his back, Fargo pressed on, hoping to find a place where he and the horse could curl up against the lee side of the bank. Maybe they'd reach the river, where the brush and cottonwoods could take some of the sting out of the wind. Of course, this brutal onslaught might just topple one of those trees over and smash him, but Fargo was past worrying about what might happen. He knew damn well what would happen —plugged nose and mouth, followed by a grave inside a brand-new dune—if he didn't get to some sort of shelter.

He still didn't dare open his eyes, not unless he wanted them clawed away by talons of grit. But Fargo sensed that he was going in the right direction. He could lift his feet without feeling the full force of the wind against his boots. So they had dropped that far, and he kept stepping, although each pace took tremendous effort because his boots were full of sand. Each shift resulted in more sand, which seemed intent on pushing his feet right out of his boots.

Now his entire lower body was free of the worst of it. He bent low and tugged the reluctant Ovaro. Because the wind sailing above had dropped several loads of sand into this depression, the footing was treacherous.

Fargo stubbed his toe against something refreshingly substantial and tumbled forward, unable to catch himself in time. His jarring downfall almost felt good. Flat on his belly, he was finally out of the gale. It still howled above him, the sky remained dark as coffee, a fine rain of grit poured down—but at least the air wasn't trying to rip off his clothes and skin.

He lay flat for a moment, savoring the relief. Then he recalled that he was still holding the Ovaro's reins, and the Ovaro was still up in the tumult. Not to mention the unknown fate of the folks he'd been riding with, presumably guiding through such hazards as desert sandstorms. He started to crawl, but the second time he stuck a wind-scourged hand forward, he was rewarded with an errant cholla spine that jammed itself under the nail of his index finger and instantly made its painful way to the quick.

His hand stung like fire, but Fargo had to use it anyway to help push himself back up on his leaden feet. He lurched forward, a step at a time, feeling his way blindly, his eyes squeezed tight, hoping with each step that he was going in the right direction. The continuous blast pushed at his torso and he stumbled often as he lifted his feet, step after goddamn step.

He couldn't help but worry about the others, but he knew that he'd never be able to do them much good unless he tended to himself first. And that was all he was able to do right now.

The Ovaro seemed more eager. Fargo realized that they had dropped far enough to be out of the worst of the wind. Just knowing that lightened his steps. He moved more quickly. The dust wasn't so intense here. Finally he could open his eyes and even make out vague features, within a few yards, anyway.

A wall of hard-packed clay loomed, almost within reach. Its top, above Fargo's head, was lost in the angry swirls of sand. But in a small area at its base, prairie grass showed between the bottom of the gulch wall and the start of a yard-high pile of wind-dropped sand. The Ovaro must have opened his eyes for long enough to notice it, too, because the horse was in as big a hurry as Fargo to get there.

The Trailsman collapsed into the spot, dropping the reins as he pressed his back against the wall and experimented with how far he could stretch his aching legs. He dropped his bandanna so he could gulp in clean air. Moments later, he untied it and used it, along with the index finger that wasn't hurting, to swab out his sand-packed ears.

All he could hear was the grumbling, shrieking sky above, and there wasn't much more to see. He rose briefly to clean the Ovaro's sand-caked nostrils and ears, then returned to his perch after grabbing a canteen. He was as comfortable as he was likely to get until this blew over, and there wasn't much he could do besides sit there and think.

Which was no pleasure. The rest of his party could be scattered across the plains already, and it was doubtful they would live through this at all. Maybe he should have halted and gotten everyone to tie together, the way that Day Woman had had her mount tied to the lead rope on the pack mules. But that would have taken time, a couple minutes at least, and Fargo had barely reached shelter as it was. He wasn't sure he'd have managed if he'd been out there any longer.

He scratched at his hair and beard, dislodging a small but intense rain of sand down onto his shoulders. The only way they would have had time to tie together would have been if he'd recognized this approaching storm earlier. But he didn't see how he could have gained more than a couple minutes on the notice he'd had, and that might not have made much difference if, at that moment, they had paused to get everybody connected.

He grunted. No matter what he had tried to do,

there just wasn't a good way to cope with a sudden wall of earth that the wind was sweeping your way. The Great Plains abounded with such difficulties—thunderstorms, tornadoes, blue norther blizzards, hailstorms, dry lighting, flash floods—and these black rollers were like all the other hazards that made prairie life so interesting and prairie deaths so frequent. About the best you could do sometimes was survive, and Fargo had so far managed to do that.

The noisy black sky overhead displayed no interest in getting quieter or lighter. The Trailsman couldn't even come up with a good guess as to what time of day it might be, but it did seem reasonable to plan on staying here for a spell, until it was possible to go somewhere else, anyway.

Glad that he hadn't put all the big canteens on one of the pack mules, Fargo grabbed one of the pair off the Ovaro and emptied it into his hat. As the horse drank greedily, he pulled off his saddle and rigging. He fished a currycomb out of one saddlebag and gave the horse a light once-over. No sense going after all the dust, because horses liked a light coating so much that they often rolled around in the dirt as they took dust baths.

The Trailsman kicked a few clumps of pincushion cactus out of the way, stomped a curious vinegaroon before it could crawl up and sting him, and spread his bedroll. There didn't seem to be much to do besides sleep as he waited this thing out.

A watch might have simplified matters when he awoke from a surprisingly sound slumber. He must have been more tired than he'd thought. The pale sky overhead could be either that of twilight or of dawn. He had to climb up out of the draw to be sure. The languid Pecos had been to the west, and the most light was over on the other side of the world. So it was morning, or would be shortly. Just as soon as he finished cleaning the grit out of his guns and breakfasting on some jerky, he would find what had happened to Gideon Hampton, Carmina, Day Woman, and six government mules.

Tracking them was out of the question. The land

had been utterly transformed since yesterday. Where there had been prairie, now there were wind-scoured bare spots. In other places, drifts and billows of sand had taken form, burying whatever sign might have survived the wind.

Fargo led the Ovaro slowly back up to the head of the draw, to where it joined the prairie. He listened intently and his lake-blue eyes devoured the region. But other than a few birds and some scurrying jackrabbits, he noticed nothing. He'd have to think this one through, and that would be mostly guesswork.

He reached the spot where he had been when he last saw the others, about a hundred yards behind him and pushing their mounts hard. They would have continued for a little ways in that direction, even after their guide had vanished in the storm. Then, what?

The mules would have taken over. They would head straight into the wind, on account of how their hair lay. Cows drifted downwind in storms, and horseflesh upwind. Although if there was any single thing you could rely on mules to do, it was to be contrary.

Fargo studied the drifts and little crescent-shaped dunes to discern the direction of the wind. It was the same as he remembered, but a man could get so addled in the midst of such a storm that it was best to double-check.

He rode south slowly, not certain what to look for. The usual signs of passage—the U-shaped marks of narrow mule shoes, the broken stems of sagebrush, plops from the mules, bent grass or cropped stems, bits of hair or clothing—would be nonexistent or meaningless after this upheaval.

After a mile or so, the land became less even. Judging by the continued evidence of yesterday's fury, the swells that were beginning to rise around the Trailsman hadn't been enough to provide any sanctuary from the storm. But going any other way would mean going uphill. It seemed safe to assume that the mules would proceed along th easiest course.

Fargo let the Ovaro pick that out as he continued, every sense alert, to search for sign. Something felt different. He realized the hairs on the back of his neck had settled down. Which could mean that he was no longer being followed by those unknown parties.

That was about the best news he could come up with during the next mile of slow riding. This depressed area was continuing to drop below the general surface of the Staked Plains, but its sides were too gentle to have offered much shelter from the wind. Eventually, Fargo knew, this half-assed ravine would drop down to the Pecos, which couldn't be more than a couple miles away.

His companions might have reached the river and sat out the storm there. Or their mules might have choked and fallen. Then the people might have suffocated, and they could be buried under one of the fresh man-high sandpiles that dotted the bleak terrain. Fargo wished he had some way of knowing.

He didn't, so he continued down the easy draw toward the river. It did get narrower, showing less effect of the brutal wind. Fargo felt encouraged. Even more cheering was a hint of drifting smoke, likely from burning greasewood, that wafted by when he rounded a bend.

Around the next bend, the walls loomed steep and narrow, and they were no longer mere cobble-studded clay, but made of rocks themselves. The bottom turned to gravel with brush rising along its flanks. Not twenty yards ahead of the Trailsman was what would be the top of a waterfall if there had been any water in the gulch. The smoke was rising from below, where he couldn't see.

There were times to be cautious, and this was one of them. He dismounted silently, pulled his Sharps carbine out of the scabbard, and padded forward, almost to the edge. He dropped low and crawled the rest of the way to the brink.

He had found the lawyer, the Apache woman, and Carmina. They sat by the little campfire. Trouble was, their hands were tied, and there were a lot of other folks nearby—Comanchero, judging by the ragged, hard-cased look of them.

7

Since nobody in the draw appeared to be in immediate danger, Fargo got comfortable in his hidden vantage and took in the situation slowly.

Perhaps a hundred yards away, Hampton, Day Woman, and Carmina all sat by the small cookfire, where a smoke-stained coffeepot bubbled. Their wrists were tied and their ankles were hobbled. But the bonds were not so tight as to cause physical pain, since the three displayed no anguish amid their understandable expressions of displeasure.

Right beside them, next to Carmina, squatted a short man, clad in a serape under a huge straw sombrero. He had to be quite strong. It wasn't just the muscles that showed when he stuck a massive arm forward to tend the fire. He easily carried enough weight to annoy a pack mule, what with his twin crossed bandoleers, a pistol on each hip, and a carbine slung over his shoulder.

Fargo recognized him as Rodrigo Baca, a mule skinner some years ago on a wagon train the Trailsman had scouted for along the Santa Fe Trail.

Fargo didn't have names to go with the hard-drawn faces of the other seven well-armed Comanchero around the camp. They came in varied sizes and colors, their outfits varied from vaquero garb to greasy buckskins, and they carried enough weaponry to outfit a fair-sized hardware store.

Fargo knew the type. In many ways, they weren't all that different from him.

They were men that didn't fit in anywhere. Some, like the burly black man tending the horses, were escaped slaves. A lot of Comanchero were half-breeds. Or else they were Indians that had been captured young and raised white. When they grew up, they were turned loose upon a world where they had no place to go: whites wouldn't accept them, and they knew nothing of the ways of their ancestors, so they couldn't go back to the tribe.

The Comanchero weren't quite as bad as their reputation for wholesale murder, raiding, theft, and looting. Nobody could have been. They were more traders than brigands. Over on the east side of the Stake Plains, bands of Comanche stole horses from the ranches of Texas. Although the Comanche measured wealth in horses, they still desired other things; guns and liquor were at the top of their wish list, and out in that vast desolation, guns and liquor were hard to come by

That's where the Comanchero came in. They would trade guns, liquor, and whatever to the Comanche in exchange for horses in Texas. The Comanchero would drive the horses across the Staked Plains to New Mexico, where they could trade the horses for guns and liquor. The other major item of this commerce was captives; those who survived being taken by the Comanche could sometimes be ransomed by the Comanchero and delivered to New Mexico.

It was a hard business in a harsh land full of rough people. The Comanchero managed by being harder, harsher, and rougher.

The three people Fargo had been traveling with weren't likely to be injured, although the women might well get passed around. The Comanchero would just take them on east and north, and see how much they could sell them for.

Unless Fargo could find a way to stop it, and that didn't look promising. He was one man against eight down there, and they could use his companions for hostages and shields. So it was time to sit still and be ready.

The light morning breeze shifted, bringing up the smoke and the scent of coffee, which got Fargo's innards to yearning. But it also carried up snatches of conversation.

"Looks like the Lord taketh away and the Lord giveth," the tallest one said. He was in buckskins and had just poured himself some coffee in a tin cup. He sipped at that and chewed down a bit of jerky before speaking again. He had to be the leader, because when he talked, the other heads snapped his way. When anyone else spoke, heads weren't in any hurry to turn.

"That cussed sandstorm comes up, and we lose every damn horse except the ones we were riding. Four hundred head, vanished. Make not a red cent off this trip, it looks like. But then these folks just wander right into where we were holed up. We'll come out with somethin'."

Someone squatting, dressed like a bull-whacker with a big-brimmed hat and his trousers tucked into the high tops of his boots, stretched his arms and grumbled. "That Apache bitch without no nose wouldn't fetch four bits in a timber camp where the men had been screwin' knotholes all winter."

"Put a sack over her head," some low voice added, coming from a lean man dressed in woolly chaps and leather vest. "They all look good enough on the other end."

"That's a fact," the bull-whacker type conceded. "The other gal there says her father, down Chihuahua way, would pay a considerable price for her if we could get word to him."

"So would half of Taos pay a good price for the *hidalgo* wench," their leader growled. "And getting word to her father would be a lot of work."

The leader turned and glared down at Gideon, who met his steely stare with one of his own.

"And this man," the leader announced, "tells us he's an agent of the United States government. He talks fancy enough, like them thieving Quaker Injun agents, so maybe he's tellin' us true."

"Be the first time anybody from the government told the truth," some voice hissed.

"That's as may be." The leader nodded. He stood near the campfire, a lean, whiplike man gesturing with his coffeecup, obviously comfortable with his command over this band of ruffians. "Point is, will this gent's Uncle Sam be willin' to ransom his wayward nephew here?"

All eyes down there were on the leader. Except for Day Woman's. Fargo had done his best to remain totally inconspicuous at his vantage, but the Apache were good at noticing things that nobody else would. She stared impassively his way. He wagged the Sharps barrel slightly and caught her slight nod. So she knew he was up there, which might simplify matters if anything happened later.

The wind shifted a bit, muffling the sounds. Fargo heard some soft rustle close by. Real close, like about a foot from his right ear. He flicked an eye that way.

A flickering tongue answered. A forked tongue, attached to about five feet of spotted, scaly snake. Just now curling most of its body, so that it would have a stable place to lunge from when it decided to strike at this warm-blooded intruder.

Fargo mulled on his options. He could certainly roll away in time and come up with a shot from his Colt. He might not kill the snake on his first shot, but there wouldn't be much doubt about who'd win.

Of course, any such sudden motion would have to attract attention down below. It could get at least three people killed; at best, they'd be hauled away.

"Gentlemen, I have observed that you are businessmen, interested in making a profit." Gideon's baritone welled up incongruously from that broomstick frame. The breeze must have shifted again.

Fargo kept his eyes glued forward. That seemed to be his only chance. Often, if a man stayed perfectly still, a snake wouldn't act. If it did strike . . . Well, Fargo had been bitten a time or two before. Snakebites weren't all as lethal as folklore sometimes made them out to be.

It would hurt like fury for a day or two, though, and he'd find it impossible to move much. If the snake bit, he might just have to lie here, in quiet teeth-clenching gut-churning pain, until he recovered enough to go find out where the Comanchero were taking the three.

The leader's voice drifted up. "That's a fact, Uncle

Sam. We are merchants of a sort. And you're the only goods we got to sell at the moment."

Sitting still and getting bit by a snake was a poor notion, Fargo decided. But anything else he might do would make matters worse. Best just to try taking his mind off it. If the reptile struck, it struck. If it didn't, it didn't.

"Very well," Hampton replied. "But you might be interested in knowing that not a hundred miles north of here, there is a large horse herd that escaped from Fort Sumner."

"You gringo shit-for-brains," Baca interjected from the other side of Carmina, "we can't sell or trade them horses to nobody. Not with the damn U.S. brand on their flanks."

Hampton shook his head. "Please, allow me to continue. These horses were captured from the Navaho and were not branded. Further, you should have no difficulty selling them, or other horses, however you acquired them, at Fort Sumner."

"The U.S. Army needs good horses," the leader rejoined. "They don't just buy any old nags you might bring in."

One bystander, likely a deserter from the cavalry on account of the blue trousers and kossuth hat he still wore, laughed at that. "No. They goes out of their way to find the worst crow bait to put you on. Sooner you get kilt that way, the sooner they can quit payin' you your thirteen dollars every month."

"Please, gentlemen," Hampton's deep and rolling voice carried enough authority so that they all simmered down, even though he was merely a captive and they were supposed to be in charge here.

"The United States government is paying a bounty of twenty dollars for each and every Indian horse delivered to Fort Sumner. The condition of the horse is immaterial, so long as it appears to be an Indian horse."

"You mean," the leader probed, "that as long as it ain't got no brand, then Uncle Sam pays twenty dollars, no questions asked?"

Hampton nodded as a silence fell while the leader mulled that over.

Fargo did some mulling on his own. He allowed his eyes to check the rightmost limits of his peripheral vision. The damn snake still sat there, all coiled up now, and staring at him, as if his ear were a delectable morsel.

Its upturned tail started to vibrate. But it didn't rattle, and in that instant Fargo realized that his companion on this ledge was just a fair-sized gopher snake, not a rattler. Their size and coloring were close, and they lived in the same places. But the gopher snake didn't have big fangs, nor was it poisonous. Fargo realized he could have avoided a lot of nervous aggravation if he'd just noticed earlier that the gopher snake's head was smaller than a rattler's.

Fargo fought off a tremendous instinct to duck or swing out at the lashing head. He steeled himself to stay put as the serpent lunged in an effort to scare him off. After three darting tries, the snake must have decided that the Trailsman was part of the scenery. The reptile leisurely uncoiled itself and slithered away, as the Comanchero leader's voice rose up toward Fargo.

"Mister, that sounds like one fine deal," the tall man was telling Hampton. "Sumner's a hell of a lot closer than Taos, where the general run of horseflesh won't fetch more'n fifteen dollars the head. We can just round up such horses as we find, take 'em in there, and sell Uncle Sam his own horses, this time around. Make another run out to the Comanche nation and sell them critters at Sumner. After all, they are Injun ponies, so we ain't exactly lyin' when we turns 'em in for the bounty. And it's gonna save us a lot of work."

From about twenty feet away, the deserter stirred and glared, but before he could voice any objections, the leader spoke to Hampton.

"Mister, that's one fine scheme. But you say you're a government man, so why is it you're tellin' us how to cheat the government?"

"Good question," Hampton shot back. "For one thing, I do not believe in this bounty scheme. The more quickly it becomes apparent that it will cost vastly more than anticipated, then the more quickly the government might abandon such a foolish policy. For another, I have every hope that, if I suggested another source of income to you and your men, you might release me and these two women from your custody."

The leader stepped back, scanned his men, and stood silent for perhaps a minute. "Fair's fair," he conceded. "But the pure fact is, you say you're a lawyer man, and I never knowed such gents to go out of their way to favor the truth. So I'll tell you what. You're going to stay with us, and if we find that what you say is right, that there are horses running loose to the north and that Sumner pays a double eagle for every head, then you'll all be free to go. If that ain't so, reckon we'll find out what you bring at the fair in Taos, providin' you live that long."

Hampton sighed and shrugged, collapsing like a spyglass being put away. "If that's how it must be."

He wasn't the only one that didn't like the notion. While all eyes were on Hampton, the deserter sprang to his feet, his pistol drawn. "We ain't goin' nowhere near no army post, now or ever," he shouted as he made sure the pistol was pointed at the leader to emphasize his point.

"Something I neglected to mention," Hampton told the group. "The army also pays a bounty for deserters."

The onetime cavalry trooper stepped back, to make sure everyone at the campsite could be covered by his huge Walker Colt. "I say we just haul Mr. Silver Tongue here and them two sluts on over to Taos and get what we can for 'em."

He had the drop on the whole camp. He couldn't shoot everybody before one of them dropped him. But the first one to move would likely die, and nobody down there appeared to be in any hurry to try that.

Their leader showed his mettle. As Day Woman whiplashed herself backward, Carmina following a moment later, the leader jumped sideways and landed in a crouch, starting to bring his gun up.

Baca wasn't any slouch, either. The short, squat

bandit rolled forward, flattening himself with his pistol before him.

Dust was barely rising from these actions when the deserter screwed up and took the time to think about which man he ought to shoot first. During his eyeblink pause, Fargo got him in the sights of his Sharps and eased the trigger.

Blood exploded in every direction from what had been the deserter's head. The battered trooper hat flew upward, propelled by a spurting geyser of gore. A crimson stump remained underneath, twisting and gushing. Just enough remained so that the man could display dying reflex. The deserter's last, and only, bullet slammed into the leader's chest.

In retaliation for his leader's fall, Baca poured four instant rounds toward the deserter's twisting torso. They looked like little red dots in front, but when the man spun and his back was visible, the soft expanding bullets had ripped him open. White glints of shattered ribs and spine showed amid hanging sinew. Like a headless chicken, he jerked and twitched for several seconds after he tumbled front-down into the dirt.

The six remaining Comanchero had their guns out, but weren't too sure what to do with them. Almost in unison, they glanced at their tall leader, who was curled up on his belly in obvious gutshot anguish. Then they looked up, toward the rising puff of smoke on the brink.

Fargo hollered down at Baca. "Hey, Rodrigo, simmer down."

Baca looked perplexed, and he didn't settle down worth mention. "Who is that who speaks to me?" he shouted up.

"Fargo. Skye Fargo."

"My old *compadre*, the Trailsman?"

"*Sí*," Fargo assured him. "Now, you men put your guns down, and we'll figure something out here."

He had the drop on them, so Baca looked agreeable to the notion of shedding some hardware. As for their leader, he wouldn't be leading again for a spell, if ever. Besides, in the ruckus, Fargo's three companions were left sitting by themselves, with nobody closer than fifteen or twenty feet. That should discourage any of the Comanchero from using them as shields.

No, it didn't. The copper-colored guy in the tight black vaquero gear might have thought he was being inconspicuous, the way he was dropping the gun on his left, where Fargo could see it, and bringing the one up on his right, even as he shuffled toward the three captives.

"Drop it," Fargo warned, but the man must have thought the Trailsman was talking to somebody else. Some folks never would understand anything except hot lead, Fargo thought sadly, but there wasn't much he could do about that except get the message across.

His leaden ounce of message plowed into the man's left arm. Had the arm not been there, it would have plowed into his ribs and killed him instantly. Instead, it stopped at the man's elbow, where the bones shattered as they absorbed the bullet's force. Hardly any blood emerged—about a good scratch's worth—but the man pinwheeled sideways.

He landed, cocked on his head, and no doubt confused, because he reached out with his left arm to push himself back up. His forearm hung limply at a bizarre angle. With dazed eyes, the vaquero stared at his useless hand, as if he might order it to work. Then he doubled in pain and slumped forward.

"Rodrigo," Fargo commanded, "you need to get these men to drop their weapons. As you can see, I'm trying very hard to be reasonable about this."

Baca looked up. *"Sí.* I try, Señor Fargo. Where do you want the guns?"

"Put them in a pile across the fire from the lawyer and the women. Do it slow, one at a time. Because any sudden moves seem to excite the hell out of my trigger finger this morning."

Baca went first, dropping his pistols, then his carbine, followed by the bandoleers, three hideout derringers, a long-bladed throwing knife, two shorter blades, and perhaps some other weapons. From this distance, it was hard to be sure.

The big black man went next, depositing a pistol and a straight-edged razor. Fargo called a halt the moment he was done.

"Carmina," he shouted, "hobble over there and pick up a knife and get yourselves cut free."

She gazed up wide-eyed, but instead of rising, she translated the order to Day Woman. She was the one Fargo would have picked for the chore, anyway, if he'd been able to holler anything that she might understand. With astonishing agility for someone who was hobbled and tied, she got a knife in her hands, bent low, sliced the bonds of her feet, then transferred the haft to her mouth. While holding that in her yellowed teeth, she lifted her hands, almost like someone praying, and cut them free.

For a moment, Fargo despaired that she might just run off. She glanced around warily, as if she were trying to determine the best escape route. But a woman who would free horses from captivity apparently thought humans deserved as good a treatment. She stepped back over and cut Carmina and the lawyer loose.

"You three grab yourselves some guns out of the pile, then step back toward me," Fargo shouted, realizing that he had some awful cramps in his legs from staying so low for so long. There wasn't any need for that now, so he rose and stretched before continuing.

"The rest of you Comanchero, go on up and drop your guns, just like the others."

While his three companions backed themselves his way, the Comanchero stood in line and complied. "Now, get away from the fire," Fargo commanded, "and drag your boss man with you—after you make sure he's disarmed. Rodrigo, you tend to that."

Fargo wasn't sure whether he could trust Rodrigo Baca to bend down and not come up shooting with one of the leader's pistols. But he knew it was a safer course than sending one of his own people. For all he could tell, the leader might be playing possum and be lying there ready to strike at any enemy that came near.

But Baca tossed two more guns into the pile, then

straightened. "Señor Fargo, he hurt bad. I move him, I kill him. You want him dead, you kill him." With that, the short but barrel-built Comanchero stepped away toward the others.

Shit, the Trailsman thought. "Who's in charge down there now?"

He didn't expect a spoken answer, but he found out what he wanted to know when all Comanchero eyes turned to Baca.

"Rodrigo, we've ridden together some, haven't we?"

The Comanchero's huge cream-colored straw sombrero bobbed with his nodding answer. *"Sí.* Perhaps that is why you have not killed all of us yet."

"Maybe so," Fargo grunted, mostly to himself. "Rodrigo, where are the mules those three were riding and packing?"

"Back with our own horses, toward the river."

Even though his own people had guns, and the Comanchero were more or less disarmed, Fargo was still hesitant about lifting his eyes enough to confirm Baca's answer. Back of a pile of saddles and tack, the mules grazed amid the Comanchero's riding horses.

"Okay, I'm coming down," the Trailsman announced. "Carmina? Hampton?"

They shouted that they were paying attention, but they had enough sense not to turn toward him. Instead, they still stood with their backs to Fargo and the short precipice, their eyes and guns pointed toward the Comanchero.

"Keep them covered while I work my way down there."

"What you plan to do, Trailsman?" Rodrigo asked as Fargo slid over the edge, feetfirst and belly to the sharp rock.

The Trailsman didn't answer for several minutes. Finding handholds and footholds along the sheer rock face occupied his full concentration. He had only about thirty feet to work down, though, before he could scramble while staying on his feet.

"What I plan," Fargo said after reaching his three companions, "is for you to give me your word, *mano a mano,* Rodrigo."

"Word as to what, Señor Fargo?"

"That you will go north from here, grab what horses you might find, and continue your normal business, just as Mr. Hampton suggested to you. That you will do that and that you will not follow us."

"Why would we want to do that, Señor Fargo?"

The sullen, vengeful stares of his Comanchero companions offered ample explanation as to why they might want to follow the Trailsman.

"Here is what will happen," Fargo announced. "As soon as it cools off a bit out here, you men will shed your clothes. We are going to ride away."

"Jesus," the black man spat. "You might as well just kill us as we stand, as to strip us, then take our guns and horses and leave us here."

Fargo grinned. "Had enough killing today. Maybe. There won't be any more of it as long as you fellows listen and do what you're told."

They were quite attentive now. Fargo continued. "Day Woman here is going to see if she can patch up your leader. She tends to injuries pretty well. I know that for a fact.

"Meanwhile, we're going to make ready to ride on. Which we'll do, carrying your clothes and guns and horses with us. About a mile or two off, you'll find your clothes. Your guns, the ones we let you keep anyway, will be sitting within five miles. The horses—well, we'll turn them loose about there, but likely you'll find them down by the Pecos. You know they'll wander to grass and water."

Rodrigo slowly smiled, his teeth glistening between a drooping mustache. "You figure that by the time we get ourselves put back together for travel, you will be long gone."

Fargo nodded. "You and I always did see eye to eye on a lot of things, Rodrigo. Wish we were on the same side this time around."

Baca shrugged philosophically. "It is indeed a pity. We were quite the team the day the Comanche raided our wagon train some summers back. Perhaps again someday we can ride together."

"Maybe it will work that way," Fargo granted. "Maybe not. But we'll both be a lot happier if I don't see you for a spell."

"I gave you my word that we would not follow you, Señor Fargo. But *por favor*, Señor Fargo, if you must take some weapons, leave me my throwing knife."

"Done," the Trailsman agreed. "You'll find it about five miles out."

8

The Sacramento Range wouldn't make much more than a wart if stacked against other mountains of the West. But these hills offered cool air, refreshing shade, and babbling creeks. That was a considerable improvement on the Staked Plains. The going was harder, though, especially along this steep, twisting path that switched from side to side of some nameless creek near the headwaters of the Rio Penasco.

Atop a government mule as he reached the dividing ridge, Fargo shifted uncomfortably while he scanned the mountainous, timbered countryside and waited for the others to arrive.

He was riding the mule because his Ovaro could use a day off. But the mule's back wasn't nearly as wide as his big pinto's, so his custom saddle would have rolled and hung upside down, seat under the mule's belly, no matter how tight he snugged the cinches.

This government McClellan saddle was much lighter than his own big saddle with its high cantle. It didn't sport much in the way of skirts, it didn't have a horn, and it really didn't have a seat worthy of the name. Instead, there was a hole, which a man's balls would have jangled down into if he'd been of a mind to ride naked.

Fargo had his trousers on, but the unfamiliar saddle was still disconcerting. It forced you to sit in a different manner and it rubbed you in different places. A man could get used to it, no doubt, but Fargo figured it would be easier just to think about how comfortable he'd feel tomorrow, when he'd be back in his own saddle.

About the time Hampton arrived, Fargo was ready

to dismount. Then a vagrant stir of dust rose a few miles to the rear. Fargo stretched and stared hard, but that was it: just a little dust. Just more damn evidence that he was being followed by somebody that was as persistent as a bounty-hunter. But only one somebody lately, since the sandstorm. From Sumner to there, he recalled, there had been two parties of pursuers.

Gideon Hampton looked that way, then turned to the Trailsman and read the consternation on his face. "Someone behind us again, Fargo?"

He nodded. "Looks that way, Hampton. Can't be totally sure, not from here. Just makes me edgy, that's all. It's bad enough traveling through Mimbreno Apache country that's perfect for ambushes."

The lean lawyer nodded in commiseration and looked back down the trail. "Well, at least the women are in sight now." He hemmed and hawed a bit before continuing. "Say, Fargo, mind if I ask you a question?"

"You just did."

Hampton chuckled. "Then I shall ask another. When we were out on the plains, you said you planned to stay east of the mountains, all the way down to Presidio on the Rio Grande. Then, after the women and I blundered our way into Comanchero hands and you rescued us, we crossed the Pecos and headed west, into the mountains. Is there a reason for this change in course, or is it just because we can enjoy shade, firewood, water, and game up here?"

"Something to that," Fargo conceded. He waved the two women off their mounts for a rest stop. "Out on the prairie, all we ran into was trouble, mostly on account of that damn bounty business. The way folks saw it, we were toting some valuable cargo in the form of those two women. And there are plenty of robbers in New Mexico Territory."

"All the way up to the Palace of the Governors in Santa Fe, judging from what I have heard," Hampton noted.

"I've heard the same myself," Fargo agreed. "If you want to get into some profitable wholesale thieving, go into politics." The Trailsman paused and wiped his brow, disturbing a cloud of mosquitoes. "But that's not important here. Another reason I switched directions was that I don't know what you might or might not have told those Comanchero about our travel plans," Fargo added. "I was hoping we'd give everybody the slip by heading up the Penasco at night. But dammit, I was wrong. Somebody's still back there."

Carmina and Day Woman were chattering away as they stepped into view, stretching their muscles and rubbing at themselves. They seemed to walk with more comfort than they rode.

Fargo grew silent and stared to the west, pulling his hat's broad brim low to shield his eyes from the descending sun. The vast valley of the Rio Grande spread before him, beneath a blue-brown haze. At the close edge, though, just under the mountains they were crossing, the land almost glowed a radiant, pearly white.

Hampton caught the brightness. Fargo answered his question before he could ask it. "Big patch of inland sand dunes there. It's peculiar sand, as white as alabaster or gypsum. We'll have to skirt them."

Then Fargo looked around the summit of the pass again. He didn't see Apache sign, and he hadn't seen any along the trail. Nor had Day Woman, according to Carmina's translations. That didn't mean a whole lot, since the Apache were damn good at covering their tracks and hiding their presence. But not finding sign was better than finding it.

Back to the east, another puff of dust rose from the trail. Who or what was back there? Fargo knew he had to find out. Which would mean leaving these three alone in Apache country while he circled back there to see what he could see. He didn't like the notion, and Hampton caught that in his expression.

"Observe that little glen down there." The lawyer pointed down the west about half a mile. "It has water and decent cover. We could stand off any attack there for a considerable period if you need to be free of our company."

"You're sure?"

"Nothing is certain save death and taxes, Fargo. But we all share your trepidation about that party to our rear. Carmina told me that during the time they were transporting you, during your recovery from the shoulder wound, there was similar evidence of a party trailing them. She and Day Woman share your concern and mine."

Fargo aimed a questioning glance at Carmina, who had to have overheard the conversation. If any concern about anything showed in her impassive thin face, Fargo sure couldn't notice it. And he was sure he would have, because it would be the first time she'd ever showed concern about anything.

Carmina said something to Day Woman, who did exhibit some animation in her reply. Fargo asked what she had said. "She say a real warrior would go back and kill those who follow him and his people."

"Then tell her I'm doing half the job tonight. I'm going back there. But I'll make no promises about killing anyone." Fargo smiled.

As the others made their way toward the promising campsite, Fargo swatted the pack mules, just to make sure they'd kick up a goodly cloud of telltale dust. He wanted whoever was back there to believe that the party had crossed the pass and was dropping down the west side.

On the way up, Fargo had been attentive, as always. He recalled an outcrop of boulders about file miles back, several hundred yards off their trail. If he'd been traveling solo or with just one other, and had wanted to stay out of sight for a night, that's the place he would have picked. He guessed other people might use the same logic.

After a day of trying to adjust to that cussed government saddle, a stroll felt good. Moving afoot with long and easy ground-eating strides, he headed back down the route he had just come up. He kept to the sides of the trail, which was coated with a forest duff that wasn't quite so prone to rise as dust was.

A problem with the edge of many trails was that tree limbs stuck out. He ducked the long-needled ponderosa easily enough, but sometimes he brushed a branch. One such branch sported a wasp nest, and when it jiggled, an annoyed cloud of insects tore after the Trailsman.

But they gave up after a few yards. Only one got a bite of him, raising a welt on the back of his neck. Once out of their territory, he had to stop and apply an impromptu mud poultice of spit-wetted trail dust. That was as good a place as any to slow down and make his way up the brush-choked hillside, then angle toward the rock outcrop that couldn't be more than a mile away.

Moving through brush, especially in these deep and descending shadows, was always a chore, and it was made even worse by the necessity of silence. About halfway up the flanking slope, Fargo almost stepped on a mottled gray-blue grouse that had been foraging around on the ground for some insects for her dinner. The hen rose, almost in his face, with a clumsy thumping clutter of wings that sounded like thunder in the evening quiet. Her ruffled departure inspired a big horned owl, perched near the shattered top of a lightning-killed lodgepole, to start hooting. Another owl, some distance away, hooted back. At least Fargo hoped it was an owl, and not an Apache signaling a friend.

A few yards ahead of the Trailsman, a big-eared doe mule deer thrashed by, with a light-stepping fawn right behind her. Two scuttling rabbits, on their way to better cover now that the hungry owls were stirring, crossed Fargo's path. Even their hushed rustling progress seemed to make an ungodly amount of noise. He had the feeling that he'd set off a general alarm hereabouts, that he might as well have hired a brass band.

"Simmer down," he told himself as he stood, still as any tree trunk. "Fact is, it's evening, when lots of animals stir. The day ones are going to find a place to sleep, and the night ones are just getting up and about. Every outdoor place gets noisy this time of day, and all this commotion will cover any sounds you might make." Trying to believe himself, he proceeded, even more slowly and carefully than before.

The last mile took better than an hour, and Fargo had no idea whether this was worth the trouble or not.

The rock outcrop was just a guess. Whoever had been following could have found a lot of other places to pull over for the night.

But for once something went right. After checking carefully for snakes, scorpions, tarantulas, cactus, poison-oak leaves, and half a dozen other annoyances that came to mind, Fargo hunkered down, made himself as comfortable as he could, and stared down at the tiny fire in the rocks.

Some neatly stacked gear sat near it, but no people or horses were in sight. Since campfires hardly ever started themselves, Fargo figured he'd have to wait. Stars were popping out above him, and his legs were growing fearsome cramps by the time someone appeared below.

A man, dressed in usual outdoor gear, stepped in warily with an armload of twigs and branches. After halting at the edge of the light and making sure that everything looked in order, he poked a few little pieces of wood into the fire. Then he fished a skillet out of a bag, tossed in a piece of bacon fat, and got it heating.

A couple minutes later, a companion appeared from the other side of the rocks. He toted a dead cottontail, which he began to skin and clean after getting a nod from his companion.

The tiny fire—no bigger than a man's hat—didn't provide much light. What there was flickered. Shadows twisted and bounced every which way. Fargo had to assemble mental images of the men, a piece at a time, until he could envision what they looked like, all at once in good light.

They weren't really men. They were boys, not much more than sixteen or seventeen. Their motions weren't as smooth or certain as grown men's. Though neither was as thin as, say, Hampton, they didn't look filled-out. Their shoulders stretched wide, out of proportion to the rest of their torsos, and their arms didn't bulge enough.

The orange glow of the firelight showed that the close-cropped taller one was trying to grow a mustache, but it looked more like he'd smeared his upper lip with a piece of charcoal. The shorter had blond hair that covered his ears, and didn't seem to be quite as dark. Both had pointed chins, puffy cheeks, and deep-set eyes. So, despite the difference in coloring, Fargo figured them to be at least cousins, and likely brothers.

Only after a meal in silence—the loudest sound was either the crackling of the fire or the growling in Fargo's empty innards—did either of them speak.

"Reckon we found his trail again," the shorter said. "Wasn't easy. That jasper's pretty smooth, switching routes after the sandstorm like that."

"He's goddamn smooth for a murdersome son of a bitch," the taller grunted.

These boys hadn't been among the Comanchero back on the other side of the Pecos, Fargo was certain. But maybe they had some sort of connection to that band. Why else would they be referring to the man they were trailing—Skye Fargo—as a murderer?

The short fair-haired one got the last morsel of meat off a rabbit leg before tossing the bone into the fire. "We know he's got to be camped just over the top. You saw the dust and smoke, too. He's got sloppy, must not think we're still on his tail. So what say we just go up there tonight and get this done?"

If that was their plan, they wouldn't leave their fire alive. Fargo had his Colt with him to ensure that.

The taller one shook his head. "Because them that he's with might get killed in the process. Our beef's with him, not with the others. We wait till we can find him alone, wherever that is. That's what we agreed when we started after him, and that's how it's going to stay."

"Shit," the short boy spat. "I reckon that's right. But this is getting mighty tedious. Our horses is damn near as wore out as I feel. And this is Apache country, too, ain't it?"

"Everywhere we been, pretty much, is Apache territory, from yonder by Fort Yuma, across the Sonora, up into the mountains, out toward the Llano Estacado, back up here—shit, they're everywhere."

Their talk drifted off toward the usual trail complaints. When they began to stir—one to tend the horses that were off behind some boulders, and the other to spread their bedrolls—Fargo rose silently and removed himself. He could have killed them, he knew. But if they were part of a family bent on vengeance, for whatever reasons, then there would just be more family after him. It would be best to find out just what they were up to before he took any action.

He headed back up to his own camp, moving slowly and silently through the darkness. This might have come naturally to wild animals, but it took effort for the Trailsman. To keep himself from moving with undue haste, he pondered on the boys back up in the rocks.

It was obvious what they were up to. They were trailing Skye Fargo, and whenever they could find him alone, they intended to kill him. They had been shading the Trailsman for how long? Since Fort Yuma?

That didn't make sense. Yuma was far to the west. It was the crossing of the Colorado River that took you into California, that's how far west it was. Fargo hadn't been anywhere near Yuma for better than a year. Make that two years, he recollected. This wasn't adding up.

Thanks to that addled spell after the Apache bullet that nearly tore his right arm off, Fargo's memory of recent travels was muddled. He sorted through it. He'd been riding away from Persnickety Springs in a fearsome hurry, hoping to escape the Apache. He'd been hit, hit hard, but he'd pressed on, collapsing eventually.

Then Day Woman and Carmina had found him. But Hampton had said that Carmina had claimed that someone was following them while they hauled Fargo, sleeping and moaning and delirious, on a travois across a goodly chunk of the Southwest. And Fargo knew for a fact that somebody had been behind them from the time he had come to, out on the prairie east of Glorieta Pass.

That was long before the run-in with the Comanchero. The boys certainly weren't Apache. So why did they think they were trailing a murderer when they trailed Fargo?

He shrugged. He was back down to the regular trail by the creek, which offered easier going, especially by starlight. And at night he didn't have to be so mindful about stirring up dust. With long steps, he proceeded up the pass toward his own camp.

You've shot a lot of men, Fargo reasoned to himself. Best as you know, they all had it coming. But their kinfolk might not have seen it that way. Could be these boys are out for vengeance over something that happened long ago.

But even if that were so, why were they talking about picking up his trail way over by Yuma, where he hadn't been for a long spell?

Fargo moved his attention back to the trail. Especially to a rounded boulder on its side, one that hadn't been there under the light of the sun. He stepped on toward it, drawing his Colt when he got within twenty paces.

He had suspected correctly. The smooth rock was breathing. It was a hunkered-up Apache brave. This could be just one scout, checking activity along here. That sometimes happened. But there was really no telling just how many Indians might be lurking hereabouts, sitting still in the darkness, ready to pounce. So the Trailsman stepped to where he had his back to a tree, with a downed trunk providing some cover should he need to duck in a hurry.

"Yo," he called. Nothing happened. "Hey, is this a good day to die?" he shouted.

Finally the warrior stirred a trifle. "Yo," he hissed back.

"Habla ingles?" Fargo questioned. A lot more Apache spoke Spanish than spoke English, so it wasn't quite so foolish as it seemed to be asking an Indian in Spanish if he spoke English.

"Yes," came the breathy reply.

"Then come over here. We'll talk. Or stay there and you die."

The last thing Fargo wanted was to start shooting in the dark, when there might be two dozen warriors secreted along this trail. But Indians were like a lot of wild creatures: you got some respect from them if you acted a lot less fearful than you felt.

Clad only in a breechcloth, the warrior, considerably shorter than the Trailsman but broad-shouldered and looking powerful, rose and stepped toward Fargo. He held a scalping knife in his right hand. It didn't seem poised for immediate action, but the Trailsman knew better.

"I am called Skye Fargo. What are you called?"

"If you are also called the Trailsman, then I know of you. Your medicine is powerful. My people speak well of you."

"My heart soars to hear that from one of the people," Fargo replied. "But again I must ask, what is this person called that I am speaking to?"

"My people call me Goy-ah-kla. Your people would say I am called Man Who Yawns. My enemies, the Mexicans who butchered my wife, Alope, and my three sons, have many other names for me—*ladrón, bandido, asesino, invasor.* Sometimes they call me Geronimo, though I know not why."

"I have heard something of you, too, that you are a strong warrior," the Trailsman answered. Actually, none of those three names was at all familiar. But it didn't cost anything to be polite and a little flattersome here. Because as nearly as he could tell, he and One Who Yawns weren't enemies at the moment, and Fargo didn't need any more enemies.

It was surprising, considering what you generally heard, but some Apache bands got along tolerably well with English-speaking white folks. That was because the Apache had about three hundred years of grudges to settle with the Mexicans, who had been the first to invade their traditional homelands in the rugged country along both sides of the Rio Grande.

The Mexicans saw it differently. The Apache raided villages, ranchos, and haciendas throughout the north part of Mexico. That's how Carmina had ended up in Indian hands when she was but a girl of twelve.

One result of this long-standing war between the Mexicans and certain Apache bands was that a tall, blue-eyed man like the Trailsman was not automatically regarded by some Apache as an enemy.

One Who Yawns confirmed that. "You stand too close to the sky, Trailsman, to be one of my enemies. I will fight you if you wish, of course."

Fargo shrugged. "If it's all the same to you, I'd rather parley. Are the people of my band safe in their camp?"

The Indian nodded. "If it is the camp just over the hill, they are safe. The lodgepole man who talks too much. The Woman of my People Who Was Caught in Adultery. The slender woman that I should kill because she is of Mexico. They are all good when I spied them. What brings you to this land?"

Dawn, travel got complicated hereabouts. Gideon Hampton was a city man who did his best and didn't complain, but he still wasn't exactly the man Fargo would have picked to side him in this country. The lawyer just didn't have much trail sense. Then again, Hampton's smooth tongue and commission from President Lincoln had helped considerable when they'd been forced to deal with the army.

Carmina's Mexican citizenship had also come in useful back at Sumner. But now she was going to make things real tricky when going through Apache country. Day Woman had been a lure to bounty-hunters before, although she might be a blessing now. Everybody with him seemed to carry both benefits and problems, and just which was which seemed to change day by day, if not moment by moment.

"We are bound for Chihuahua," Fargo finally replied. "I would like it if your people gave us safe passage. But we will go there, either way."

The Indian shrugged. "My people are far away, to the south and west, where there is much fighting. I came east alone, searching a safer place for my people."

"Don't go much farther east," the Trailsman cautioned. He explained the bounties and the consequent difficulties any Apaches would face anywhere within convenient reach of Fort Sumner.

Geronimo took his time in replying. "Your people must have their hearts set upon the path of becoming the enemies of my people. But hear me, that is not the path my people wish to walk. Our enemies are the Mexicans."

"Wasn't my idea," Fargo agreed. "And it hasn't happened yet, even if it looks like it's bound to. So let's figure out just how you and I stand now."

"It is simple," One Who Yawns said after taking a moment to lift a big hand to his open mouth while he lived up to his name. "You stand there with a gun. I stand here alone. If I return to my people in the west, I will tell them that you are a good man with a strong heart. You could have sold my sister's scalp to the Blue Sleeves for gold, and you did not. You are not like most white-eyes, who would do anything for gold. So you and your band should ride in peace among my people, even if one of your band is a Mexican who should be killed."

"I would like to tell my people to the east the same thing about you, that you are a man of good heart who rides in peace," Fargo replied. "But I am not a chief, and so they will not hear me."

The Indian nodded. "I am not a chief, either. Perhaps someday I will be a great leader of my people, as Mangas Coloradas was."

Mangas Coloradas—Red Sleeves—had carried on a fearsome war against the Mexicans. Gringos, too, as Fargo recalled, but there was no sense bringing that up at the moment. Not if Geronimo wanted to be friendly. Instead, Fargo inquired about conditions to the south and west, the way One Who Yawns had come.

"There is much fighting everywhere. Especially below the border. The Mexicans are doing my people's work. They are busy killing Mexicans. Not raiding like always, but armies in uniforms doing battle with each other. Mind you, Trailsman, I have not seen this with my own eyes. But it is what people who usually tell truth have told me."

Mexico didn't sound any too promising. But in that part of the world, fighting was a lot like thunderstorms. It came and went, and it might well be gone by the time Fargo got there.

If he got there with his party. Because when he approached what he thought was his camp, things didn't look quite right. For good reason. He crept closer and realized that, despite distant appearances, nobody was in the bedrolls scattered around the dying embers of the campfire.

Shit. Every time those three got out of sight, they found some way to get into trouble. Geronimo must have been lying about traveling solo, for it sure looked as though Hampton, Carmina, and Day Woman had been spirited away by Apaches.

9

Under stars that looked a lot brighter than they really were, Fargo peered across the deserted campsite. He strained for signs of a struggle, a disturbance, anything. The harder he looked, the less he saw. He couldn't hear anything except his own angry pulse sounding in his ears. He realized this wouldn't work, and forced himself to relax with a few deep breaths.

That was better. Some muffled but regular sounds emerged from the trees. Hand on his Colt, he stepped that way gingerly, trying not to make noise. That was laborious, since he had to fight through the sharp-stemmed willows that lined the tiny creek to make his way across.

But the sounds were more distinct over here. The low rumble had to be Hampton's annoying snore, and the peculiar hiss belonged to Day Woman's respiration, which sounded odd because she had but a stump of a nose. Feeling better about his discoveries so far, the Trailsman pushed between two close aspen saplings.

In the darkness of night, it took him a minute or two to be sure just what he was seeing. His three companions were all snuggled up together in one makeshift bedroll assembled from wool saddle blankets and canvas pack covers. Hampton lay in the middle, snoring serenely with a woman cuddling him on each side.

Fargo was of half a mind to step closer and see if the lawyer was sporting a big happy grin. But he thought better of the notion and padded across the creek. He rustled a couple of blankets, then moved over by the horses, where he got as comfortable as he could for what was left of the night.

Which didn't seem like nearly enough when he

awoke, rubbing sunshine and grogginess out of his eyes. Over morning coffee, he confirmed what he had suspected: that Apache he'd met last night, One Who Yawns, had passed their camp; no one noticed his sneaky and silent passage except Day Woman, who told Carmina, who told Hampton.

"Since there were hostiles about," he explained to Fargo, "it appeared that the most reasonable course was to establish a sham camp, while we slept elsewhere. That way, if we were attacked, the attackers would very probably strike there first, which might provide us with enough warning—"

"Say no more," Fargo interjected. "It's an old trick."

Upon realizing that he hadn't invented this ruse, Hampton looked a bit crestfallen. "You mean to say that this has been done before?"

"Likely since Methuselah started shaving," Fargo pointed out. "But even if you weren't the first to think of it, you were thinking right."

The compliment improved Hampton's disposition. Fargo's improved mightily the next night, on the edge of the dunes of white sand, when Day Woman returned to his bedroll. For the next three days, they kept to the edge of the road that led to El Paso, avoiding confrontations. And for those three days, Fargo generally managed to dismiss the edgy feeling that he always had when he knew he was being followed.

He knew he was more than a match for the two boys back there. It was what he didn't know that was troublesome: why were they so angry with him that they had followed him across better than a thousand miles of rough country, much of it desert, at the height of summer? Why did they think they had started on his tail at Yuma when he hadn't been anywhere near Yuma?

The day came when it was time to get some answers. They were camped along the cottonwoods that lined the summer-shallow Rio Grande, four or five miles upriver from El Paso. Their spot was a good mile from the road, where accidental discovery was about as likely as a case of frostbite on one of these blistering afternoons.

So the womenfolk would likely be safe enough if they stayed put.

Hampton had his own reasons for leaving camp that morning. "Fargo, there are certain formalities that we must observe before entering the Republic of Mexico," he began.

"Such as taking off our boots before we wade across the river?" Fargo wondered.

"Were it that simple," the lawyer rejoined. "But it cannot be, because I am on an official mission, even if my real mission—determining what might be occurring in northern Mexico—is not the same as my official mission—the examination of certain documents relating to a land grant. We need to enter Mexico properly and legally, if that is at all possible. I am not certain, but that may mean we need entry documents, which is why I intend to see the Mexican consulate in El Paso, or else the customs authorities across the river."

Fargo shrugged. "If that's what you need to do, that's okay by me, as long as you handle the paperwork."

"That is my specialty, after all," the lawyer pointed out. "And I anticipate my task might be simplified if I went to El Paso by myself. I shall have to explain about the land-grant boundary question, and I can say you are my guide. Regarding Carmina, well, it is a treaty obligation to return her to her home, so I should be able to explain that satisfactorily. But as for Day Woman, I very much doubt that the Mexicans would welcome any new Apaches."

He sighed before continuing. "I'll come up with something. Perhaps I can say she is Carmina's servant. At least we won't have to worry about bounty-hungry soldiers down there, anyway."

Fargo started laughing without much humor. Hampton asked why.

"Because, unless they've changed things, the Mex government is paying a bigger bounty on Apaches than ours is. Last I heard, an Apache scalp would fetch you just twenty-five dollars at Fort Tucson. Get into Mexico, and they'll pay you about three hundred dollars for the same chunk of hair."

The lawyer's face contorted as he whistled. "Damnation. Is there nowhere that she would be safe?"

"With us is about it, I reckon," Fargo said after due thought. "Anybody else might be able to pass as something besides Apache. But she'll always look Apache, on account of that missing nose."

The question had to come up sooner or later, so Hampton asked it now. Fargo explained that the Apache cut off the noses of women caught in adultery. The lawyer said it was a good thing that civilized Americans in distant Washington didn't do that, or else most of Congress would have flat faces and lack the ability to smell.

Hampton rode for El Paso, and Fargo headed upstream on an errand of his own.

He rode in the sandy shallows along the east bank of the Rio Grande. The going was clear, yet the riparian brush and looming cottonwoods provided cover close at hand.

The Trailsman had seen the tiny puffs of dust in the low light of yesterday's sunset. He knew just where to go, to persuade those persistent boys that they were barking up the wrong tree. Of course, the boys might decide to match their gun-handling skills against his, instead of listening. But Fargo had no doubt about the outcome if they made that foolish decision.

The Ovaro seemed to enjoy splashing in the shallow, muddy water. With a steady trot, and no quicksand or deep mud to slow them down, Fargo reckoned he was less than a mile from them when the first shot rang out from somewhere along the far bank.

Fargo rolled down toward the near bank. It meant dismounting on the wrong side of his horse, but the Ovaro didn't seem to mind. On the way, the Trailsman grabbed the Sharps. With his horse still between him and the source of that shot, Fargo leapt for the bank.

He didn't get there on his first bound. His right boot started down and just kept going as the rest of him followed. Suddenly he was stuck in the Rio Grande.

Viscous mud oozed up around his thighs. When he tried to lift a foot, the mud pulled even worse. The riverbed muck was softer than the jaws of a bear trap, but just as efficient at clamping down and refusing to let go.

The Ovaro had trotted on, so there wasn't anything between the Trailsman and the next bullet that came his way. It whistled in low, striking the water a few yards in front of him. Like a flat stone, it skipped across the surface, leaving expanding rings in its wake before it struck the shore.

An astonishing amount of greenery thrived across the river. Fargo saw the puff of gray-blue powder smoke drifting up and away. But he couldn't tell just where it had started. Whoever was shooting at him was hunkered in good cover. Though there had to be a rifle barrel over there somewhere, there was also a plentitude of sticks and branches. Even his keen eyes couldn't decide which of the two dozen possibilities was the real rifle.

Fargo didn't want to just stand there until the ambusher finally figured out the range. He shouldered his Sharps and aimed it toward a likely spot. The hidden shooter would have to see that and perhaps start thinking about it. The pointed rifle wouldn't bother an experienced man with his mind on his work, but a boy could well get flustered. The boy would have even more trouble aiming straight. He'd shoot too much and give his position away to the Trailsman. And then he'd be as good as dead, if Fargo stayed alive long enough to take him out.

During the ominous silence as he stood there, staring down the sights of his Sharps, Fargo remembered that there had been two boys who planned to shoot him as soon as they found him by himself. He was about as alone as a man could get right now. Where was the other boy? Perched somewhere nearby, even now getting ready to shoot at him, whose eyes were riveted elsewhere?

Snap. Bang. Fargo ducked as best he could, keeping his shoulders and the Sharps above water. He whirled his torso toward the sound, to the upstream. No smoke.

But a chunk of wood was drifting his way, and a fresh tree snag in the river wasn't quite as big as it had been. The noise had just been a snapping branch.

The next one wasn't, though. It came from the same old place, and if Fargo hadn't ducked for the other sharp sound, this bullet would have caught him square between the eyes. It hissed by, just overhead.

Now he saw precisely which one of the sticklike things over there was the one to be concerned about. Just under the rising smoke, it was slowly sliding back into the luxuriant leaves. Fargo estimated the range at one hundred and fifty yards, moved his sights accordingly, and softly squeezed the trigger.

This had to be a good shot. Miss now, and the bushwhacker could sidle over to try again. One of his efforts might succeed and Fargo wouldn't get another chance on this earth.

He knew he had hit his unseen target when the barrel fell suddenly, as if it had been dropped. Above the ripple of the river, he heard a grunt, followed by a little thrashing in the brush.

That was an improvement, for certain, but Fargo still wasn't comfortable. He remained stuck in the mud, with nothing nearby to grab for purchase to get out. So he was still an easy target. The boy he'd just shot might not be out for good; if it was a flesh wound, then he could resume firing at any time. And, dammit, there had been two boys traveling together. Whether they were together or apart at the moment, at least one of them would still be functioning.

But perching in this more-or-less crouch, with water up to his armpits, was getting tedious. Fargo thought to reload the Sharps, then realized that all its paper cartridges were in a pocket that had been immersed in the Rio Grande for the past few minutes. His Colt was soaked just as thoroughly into uselessness. And if he could reach the throwing knife he kept in his boot, he wouldn't be stuck here feeling like a target.

He straightened. The effort made him sink a bit deeper. The muck was now almost to his crotch. He momentarily wondered if there were any snapping turtles in the Rio Grande, then looked to see if the dropped gun on the far shore had moved. It hadn't. He whistled for the Ovaro.

Just in front of Fargo, the footing was gravel, reasonably solid. From where he stood, sinking into the mud, on back to the bank, he figured there was gumbo mud beneath the water. He confirmed that suspicion when his Ovaro stepped into the water, just a couple yards upstream. The pinto acted real testy about how he was sinking up to his fetlocks.

The Trailsman muttered some words of encouragement and checked the far bank again, where the rifle still lay undisturbed.

Dammit, the Ovaro was struggling with the mire. With water lapping at his belly, the frustrated stallion's legs pumped up and down. But he wasn't making progress worth mention toward the more solid gravel bottom right in front of him. And if the horse sank much more, there would be water in the saddlebags, where Fargo kept the ammunition for his Sharps. The case was supposed to be watertight, but Fargo knew from experience that it wasn't prudent to trust your life on such suppositions.

But Fargo felt encouraged when the Ovaro gained about a yard. A little more, and he could get one hoof up on a more solid bottom. Then he could pull himself out and come around to stand on the gravel before Fargo. He figured on grabbing the saddle horn and urging the horse. He'd just have to get pulled out that way, although he might lose his boots in the process. But what the hell good would his boots do him if he stayed in this damn mud hole?

Shit. Low to the ground, under the brush over there, an arm and hand were reaching forward. Some fresh blood stained the arm of the cotton shirt, but that wasn't much consolation. If the probing hand found that rifle and fetched it back, Fargo's life expectancy could be measured in minutes.

"C'mon, dammit," Fargo muttered to the Ovaro. The horse lunged forward and tried to kick up its rear feet. They didn't rise enough to matter, and all that it really accomplished was to shift the horse's weight so that his front hooves sunk even deeper.

If the horse would just rear back, Fargo realized, then the stallion could free his front hooves and stretch them forward enough for some tolerable footing.

But how was he supposed to persuade the horse to move? The horse was upstream and the long reins were hanging over the saddle. If they dropped, they'd trail in the current. Fargo could grab them and maybe he could figure out something from there.

Fargo slapped his hand across the muddy water, throwing a spray into the Ovaro's strained face. Perturbed, the horse shook all over like a wet dog. The reins started to slip.

The Trailsman looked up and saw that the gun on the far bank was sliding back into the bushes. He doubted that the rifle was doing this all on its own. Shit. Whoever was over there wasn't all that great a shot, but if you had lots of time, ample ammunition, and a target that didn't move, just about anybody could get the job done, great shot or not.

Another big splash inspired the Ovaro to some more angry trembling, enough for the reins to fall. The brown leather straps tumbled into the brown water. As much as he could, Fargo lunged that way, shoulders going down, his arms flailing in search of the reins.

He caught one. No, it was something slimy. He let that go and finally grabbed some leather with his left hand. He grabbed it so enthusiastically that he jerked it, sending the distant bit up into the Ovaro's windpipe. The pained and confused horse followed his instincts and reared up. One mud-coated dripping front hoof even broke the surface.

The forward-pressing Ovaro now had something solid under at least one foot. Figuring the horse could tend to the rest, Fargo examined the far bank. The gun wasn't visible at all now.

Wrong. He finally did see it. The muzzle was about six inches off the ground, where a prone man might be holding it, and it was pointed Fargo's way, although it was wagging a bit. Whenever the motion stopped, the trigger would be squeezed.

Before that happened, the heaving Ovaro came

around, with his broad side between the Trailsman and the ambusher. Maybe it was unfair to persuade the pinto to go to all that work just so he would end up being the target rather than Fargo. That was bad enough, though he figured he'd rather have the horse for a barrier. Even worse was that if the Ovaro caught a bullet and tumbled, Fargo was dead in the water anyway without the Ovaro's help to pull him out of the clutching mud.

The Trailsman leaned forward for the saddle horn at his fingertips. Just an inch or so, and he'd be able to get a grip. But he wasn't getting that inch. And any second now, the Ovaro would be shot. He angrily jerked at the close stirrup. But, dammit, he'd cinched up so well that there wasn't enough give left to roll the saddle his way.

Just to see what was going on over there, Fargo stuck his head down a bit and leaned left, so that he could peek out from under the Ovaro's neck. The muzzle moved slightly, and Fargo had his head back in before the bullet came, whistling harmlessly past where his head had just been.

Obviously, the ambusher didn't want to harm the Ovaro if it was possible not to. He just wanted Fargo out of the picture. The boy probably figured, reasonably enough, that if he waited long enough, he'd get his easy shot at the Trailsman.

After deciding on that, Fargo figured he had time while the horse stood before him. He could reach a saddlebag, which he opened. He pulled out a bandanna and swabbed the action on his Sharps. Then he got a dry cartridge and loaded it.

He urged the Ovaro to step forward, downstream, for just a bit. That way, he could lean to his right and see out. When he leaned, he had the Sharps on his shoulder, and as soon as there was room, he brought it down and fired, then straightened instantly to get back behind the Ovaro.

The snap shot was to make the bushwhacker a little more thoughtful. Fargo didn't figure he'd hit anything, and besides, he found himself too busy to check further.

After all the other annoyances today, the Ovaro had

reached the limit of his equine patience. When the Sharps thundered and the powder flash singed his rear end, the Ovaro decided to go somewhere else, just as fast as possible.

Fargo still had the reins looped in his left hand, so the horse wasn't going far without him. For an agonizing moment that seemed like years, it was a struggle between the Ovaro's strength and the suction of the mud. All Fargo could do was clench up his toes inside his boots. He hoped he could keep his footgear. He'd need his boots if he lived through this bone-stretching, joint-wrenching act of being the rope in a game of tug-of-war.

With what sounded like the smack of a passionate kiss between giants, Fargo popped out of the muck. His feet were so beslimed that he couldn't tell whether he'd kept his boots or lost them. But he had other things to worry about, like holding on and staying afloat while he got hauled through the water. The big pinto was in a considerable hurry, and those bullets splashing around back here just seemed to encourage him.

Fargo didn't see any reason to change the arrangements until they rounded a bend, thirty yards downstream and out of sight of the ambusher. Then he persuaded the horse to halt, so that he could pull himself up into his saddle. They made it to the bushwhacker's side of the river, clambering through the streamside willows.

The Trailsman knew his opponent was wounded, so he figured time might be on his side for a change. He swung out of his saddle and marveled that he still had his boots. They were full of mud and water, though; every step required heavy lifting and his feet squished and sloshed.

Wearily, he sat down and pulled his boots off. He was emptying the second one when the Ovaro tensed and the brush rustled. Reaching instinctively for his Colt, Fargo turned toward the sound.

The checked walnut grips of his big revolver were about as slippery as a bar of wet soap, and just about as useful in a fight. Which was coming, because the bleeding, wounded man who lumbered toward the Trailsman was obviously not of a peaceful frame of mind. He wasn't one of the boys, not unless one had managed to grow a chest-length beard with a few gray streaks in less than a fortnight.

The bearded man had taken Fargo's first bullet in his side. The second one must have missed, for he didn't see any other wounds as excited flies buzzed around the congealed blood. The big man wasn't walking all that well—he staggered from foot to foot like a bear going upright—but he did seem perfectly capable of pulling the trigger on the big Remington revolver in his right hand.

As the man continued his ponderous approach, Fargo let go of his useless revolver and returned to his earlier chore of cleaning out his right boot.

"Listen up, Fargo," the man grunted as he came within a dozen paces.

"I'm all ears, Sam," the Trailsman replied, his voice calmer than he felt. "What brings you down this way?"

"You knows goddamn well, Fargo. You fucked me out of some bounty money. Then, as if that ain't enough, you and that highfalutin lawyer friend of yourn pulled some kind of strings, and I lost my job scoutin' for the cavalry."

Fargo shrugged. "It was bound to happen sooner or later, Sam. Scouting jobs come and go. I know that well, since I've done them a few times myself."

Sam bristled and tried to coax some more authority into his crackling voice, so that the Trailsman might take him more seriously. "Fargo, damn it, I ain't takin' that from you."

"Seems like you already have."

"Taken all I'm gonna take, that's for sure. You thought you could sneak out of Sumner after arrangin' for me to get my ass fired, didn't you? Well, I come after you."

That explained why there had been, from time to time, evidence that two parties were at the Trailsman's rear: those two vengeful boys were one dust puff, and Sam was the other.

Sam drew a labored breath and went on. "You

damn near did give me the slip in the sandstorm. But I run across a talkative band of Comanchero out rounding up horses, and they told me where they'd met up with you. Made a big loop around that spot by the Pecos and found your sign headed west into the hills."

After hearing that, Fargo felt better about human nature. Rodrigo Baca had promised not to follow the Trailsman, and the man hadn't.

"You run across two boys during your travels?" Fargo inquired as he scraped at his muddy boot heel with a stick.

Cimarron Sam shook his head. "Never seen 'em. But there was sign that others was followin' you. Was that them?"

"Like as not." Fargo lifted his eyes to meet Sam's. "Guess there's a lot of folks following me around these days I must be real popular."

Sam grunted, "Well, I got to you first. You shit all over me, Fargo, and it's time for you to pay."

"What do you reckon I owe? I don't remember owing you much of anything."

"You can think about it while you're dying here, Fargo. Seems that I've got a gun, and you don't. So I'll give you a few bullets to remember me by—couple in the legs, smash an arm or two. Then I'm going to ride off on that fine horse of yours. You'll be layin' here dyin', hard and slow, with flies and other vermin swarmin' around you. Mayhaps then you'll know whether we're even or not."

Fargo's right hand shifted inside the boot as he replied, his voice low and measured.

"Gee, Sam, I've had enough chance to study on things already. And I ought to make it clear to you that I'm sorry, really sorry."

Sam emitted what Fargo supposed was a laugh. "Sorry about what, Fargo?"

"Sorry I didn't kill you when I had a chance before."

The lined face drew into an eager tight-lipped smile. "Damn right you should be sorry."

Fargo's hand came out of the boot, holding his throwing knife. Before Sam could react, the Trailsman's arm swung like a whiplash.

Cimarron Sam looked surprised at the motion, and even more surprised when he looked down at his chest and saw the handle sticking out, a pool of blood forming at its base. He lifted his eyes and pulled the trigger.

Had Fargo remained in place, the bullet might have caused some damage. But with the cast of the knife, he had crawfished, then lunged for the Ovaro. Maybe it was disrespectful, but he felt more comfortable sitting in his saddle while watching the old miscreant draw his last breaths.

10

The man with the mustache sat erect in his saddle. His polished brass buttons contrasted sharply with the dust-tinged blue of his uniform. He appeared to be the officer in charge of this detachment of the Mexican army, although his dozen men didn't much resemble soldiers. Dressed sensibly for ranging in the desert, they carried a variety of weapons and looked like a band of Comanchero.

In tolerable English, he introduced himself as Sergeant Federico Gómez. He explained that he and his men had surrounded and accosted the Trailsman's party, amid some tedious sand dunes that sprawled about a day's ride south of the border, because he had to see whether their papers were in order.

Fargo was of a mind to see whether his pistol was in order. But Gideon Hampton had already assured him that he had taken care of all that back in El Paso del Norte. That was the Mexican city on the south side of the river, just across from the American settlement, which was plain old El Paso. On that side, the river was the Rio Grande; on this side the Río Bravo.

Sergeant Gómez politely accepted the sheaf of documents that Hampton produced.

While he scanned them, Fargo sat silently, recalling paperwork problems on previous trips through here. For a lot of trips from Missouri westward along the Santa Fe Trail, Santa Fe was only the first stop. Then the caravans would proceed on down the river for another 550 miles to Chihuahua.

There was a tedious, but understandable, stop at the customs house in El Paso del Norte. Everything got inspected, and they issued a *guía*, a sort of commercial passport, and a *fractura*, which listed everything you were toting.

After you crossed the Río Bravo officially, matters got worse. You could get stopped anywhere, and you were required to halt at every settlement and check in. If there was an "i" that wasn't dotted or a "t" that wasn't crossed, then if you were lucky, they'd just confiscate your cargo. If you weren't fortunate, you could learn all about Mexican jails.

If you tried to slip around those checkpoints so as to avoid such nuisances, the Mexican authorities got down-right surly when they found you anywhere off the usual route.

Now Gómez began to read aloud in Spanish, while several of his men examined the Trailsman's mule train and confirmed that all was as listed. Fargo couldn't see why Gómez would care that they were toting a lot of water aboard two intestine-wrapped mules, and he figured the two jugs of whiskey were his business, not theirs.

Gómez looked up and stared at Hampton, his brown eyes drawn. *"Señor,* forgive me if I do not speak correctly, but it does not appear that you are visiting our country for to trade. You bear no trade goods, and no trading caravan would be this small. You need many hands to defend yourselves when the Apache or Comanche strike, as they often do here, despite the efforts of my brave men. So for why are you here?"

Fargo was content to let Hampton do the talking. The lanky lawyer shifted, took off his hat, and fanned himself, then replaced it before replying. "Sergeant Gómez, I believe it was stated upon one of the documents."

Gómez nodded in a way that indicated that he had read all about it. He just wanted to see whether Hampton was telling the same story as the papers.

"I am an American attorney," Hampton explained, "bound for the City of Chihuahua to examine the records pertaining to a land grant issued in 1821, up in what is now Colorado Territory. By treaty, our nation honors those grants, but the boundaries are in dispute."

The sergeant smiled. "That is not unknown, even

here," he agreed. "And who are these others?" His eyes shifted around, eventually joining his soldiers' target. Ever since they'd met, the men had been staring at Day Woman's flowing, fresh-washed hair and her noseless face. They knew an Apache bounty when they saw one.

Hampton gestured toward the Trailsman. "This is Mr. Skye Fargo, whom I have engaged as my guide."

Gómez muttered something before looking back at the other two riders in their party. "The women?" It sounded like an order, not a question.

"Señorita Carmina María Dolores Gallegos y Hernández is a citizen of your nation who was abducted some years ago by savage tribes and carried to the United States. As you must know, Sergeant, we have an obligation under international law to return her to her home."

"Or to the nearest Mexican authorities." Gómez smiled. "Which would be me and my men, would it not? And what of the other woman, the one who lost her nose somewhere, perhaps when she was washing her hair with the other Apache?"

Hampton shrugged. "She is the *señorita*'s ladyservant, another citizen of your nation whom we are returning to her home." He tried to sound convincing, but Fargo could tell the lawyer wasn't doing a good job of it.

The disbelieving look on Gómez's tan face just got more intense. He looked around at his men, giving them nods that were almost imperceptible. They tensed. Any second now, the showdown would come.

"Now that all is in order, we should like to proceed," Hampton bluffed.

Gómez looked down at the top paper again. "Alas for you, *señor,* all is not in order. For you see, these documents are not official."

"You confuse me," Hampton countered. "Are they not signed and sealed properly by a representative of your government?"

"The make-believe government of that scheming Indio peasant, Benito Juárez . . ." Gómez turned his head and spat emphatically into the sand. "That pretender and his deluded followers are not the true government of Mexico. My men and I, we serve the true leader of Mexico, General Patricio Malgaves. Soon will dawn the day that we shall liberate El Paso del Norte from the Juarista rabble."

Shit. Not that a man couldn't get himself killed easy north of the border. But at least on the American side, bandits were just that. They didn't ride around pretending to be soldiers. Or maybe this was some kind of civil war in progress.

Hampton took his time digesting the announcement. They had been in Mexico for less than two days, and already he'd have plenty to report about disturbed and confused conditions hereabouts. If he lived to make the report . . .

His hat brim low and his eyes mere slits, Fargo studied the situation. They had no cover. They were surrounded by edgy men whose trigger fingers were growing more eager by the moment. He and Hampton would be riddled within moments after the shooting started. Carmina would be preserved, if possible, so they could pass her around—a notion that bothered Fargo a lot more than it would bother her.

As for Day Woman, it depended on how long it had been since these men had been near women. If it had been a spell, they'd use her some before turning in her scalp for bounty. If they weren't real hard-up for a woman, she, too, was an immediate target. Which was too bad, Fargo thought philosophically, because she was a real tiger in the bedroll. Nose or not, she sure knew how to put pleasure into an evening.

Maybe it was something in Hampton's demeanor. He sat there glaring, as if he expected Gómez to issue a paper that would indicate that it was just fine with his version of the Mexican government if they continued south without further trouble.

That didn't happen, but Gómez did look more and more thoughtful as Hampton fixed him with baleful stares. The sergeant finally turned his head and flashed a conspiratorial smile to his men.

He then lifted his hands and arms in a massive shrug before addressing the travelers. "We are but soldiers, *señor,* and it is not for us to decide here. You will ride with us to our camp, right? And there General Malgaves himself can render a decision. Perhaps he will be merciful, you might hope, and he will just confiscate this contraband, but he will not otherwise punish you."

Since Hampton seemed important, with his aristocratic bearing and ostentatious manner of speech, he'd probably fetch a decent ransom. That had to be what Gómez had in mind.

Fargo glanced at the ragtag assortment of soldiers. They seemed satisfied with their commander's announcement. They really didn't look much like soldiers, though. They looked more like hard cases who enjoyed raiding, shooting, looting, raping, and plundering. This civil war with the Juárez forces was just an excuse for what they'd be doing anyway.

Fargo knew that if he and his party went along for this ride, he'd be shot as soon as they got away from the main road between El Paso and Chihuahua. But he nodded anyway when Hampton looked at him for guidance as to a reply to Gómez.

"It would be for the best, then, if you were to surrender your weapons," Gómez announced. "When firearms go off, people sometimes get hurt." He was looking hard at the Trailsman, although his men had returned to staring at Carmina.

Judging by their witless grins, they were daydreaming about her sweet, tender, ripe breasts that bobbed in breathy rhythmic motion while rising nipples formed delectable little orbs that were outlined on her calico shift. Or they were thinking about those firm, lithe thighs that were going to waste, pressed against an unfeeling saddle skirt instead of an eager man. Or that muscular rump, sized just right for a man's palm, or how her placid lips might be inspired.

This was as good a time as any. While Gómez watched intently from a dozen feet away, Fargo laid his reins carefully behind the saddle horn, then raised his hands toward the buckle of his gun belt.

His boot heels tore at the Ovaro's flanks. The big pinto lunged forward. Fighting the force of the inertia that wanted to lash him backward, Fargo snapped forward, pressing his body low, just in case Gómez tried to snap off a shot.

The Trailsman's muscular right arm swung out as he passed Gómez an instant later. His fist caught the sergeant hard and square in the belly. Gómez doubled forward and Fargo grabbed the soldier's saddle horn. The Trailsman swung out of his own saddle and landed behind Gómez.

The sergeant didn't even have time to catch his breath before he was jerked straight by the force of Fargo's left arm, clamped around his neck. The Trailsman's right hand held the Colt, its muzzle pressed into Gómez's ear.

Two of Gómez's men showed some ambition during Fargo's sudden charge. One had raised a gun toward Hampton. The lawyer wasn't much with a pistol, but he could work a carbine rapidly even while his horse was bolting forward. Hampton's snap shot hadn't been all that accurate, since he'd hit the horse instead of the soldier, but getting pinned down in the hot sand, under a writhing ton of horseflesh, wasn't exactly a pleasure, either.

The other had lunged toward Day Woman, trying to grab her in much the same way that Fargo had come upon Gómez. His hand had met her teeth. He had screamed in terror before jerking himself away. With several wrist tendons sliced by her savage bite, his hand hung limply at the end of his arm, right under a fountain of gushing blood.

Through this, Carmina had backed her mount into the huddled pack train, where she was dismounting now so she could take cover amid the mules.

Fargo was about to make an announcement about who was now in charge when he saw one husky, bearded man who wouldn't have heeded, anyway. His wide-brimmed straw sombrero dropped behind his ears as he pulled up his revolver, waving it toward either Hampton, or Gómez, or the Trailsman, who were pretty much in a line.

At the rear of that line, Fargo wasn't in much immediate danger, but Gómez had been right about one thing today: people often did get hurt when firearms were discharged. And Fargo didn't plan on being one of them. As far as he was concerned, things worked better the other way around.

His Colt dropped from Gómez's ear for long enough to send a bullet into the husky man's agitated chest, right at the tip of his beard where his neck sprouted from his torso. His head jumped up and back as the slug sliced his jugular. Bright crimson blood gushed upward in spasms for the few seconds that the man's heart continued to beat.

It was Gómez's sudden tensing right then that caught Fargo's attention. Otherwise, he might not have seen in time that another soldier, on his left where he couldn't bring the pistol around quickly, had his arm cocked. From the way he held his fingers straight, Fargo knew full well that a knife would be thrown momentarily.

The Trailsman pulled back with his left arm and twisted with all his might. All he could do was hope the horse under him would either stand still or step backward. If the critter moved forward, Fargo would be exposed.

A gunshot boomed as the needle pointed knife sailed by, about an inch above Gómez's nose. Hampton had spotted the knife-thrower. Not in time to stop the razor-edged missile, but in time to ensure that the man would never throw another one. The lawyer's shot bored a little hole on the near side of his rib cage. It was hard to tell just how big the hole was on the other side, given how much rosy mist and bits of gore were spouting out. He tumbled into the dirt as his horse took off for places unknown.

Since Hampton was coming his way, and Fargo could cover him in case somebody tried a back shot, the Trailsman checked on the women. Carmina was still among the mules, and had dismounted. She wasn't in any real danger of getting shot, although the animals were getting anxious about the overwhelming scent of fresh blood. If things didn't settle shortly, she might well get stomped, gouged, kicked, or otherwise mauled and pummeled.

Day Woman was on her way toward Carmina, followed by two men who had realized that her scalp was worth more to them off her than on her. Fargo's first shot smashed one man's elbow. He writhed and shuddered as his drawn gun dropped softly into the sand.

The other would-be bounty-collector had a carbine to his shoulder. He was about thirty yards away. Fargo's shot sailed slightly wide, although it made the man's horse rear, thus sending his shot low, into the sand at Day Woman's moccasins.

By then Hampton, whose carbine was better for that kind of work, had gotten up beside the Trailsman. Before the soldier could take another shot at Day Woman, the lawyer's bullet pierced the man square between the ears.

"Tell your men to settle down, or you are dead, Sergeant." Fargo had planned to do this in the first place, as soon as he had arrived behind Gómez, but things had just happened too fast.

Gómez strained, but all that came out was a gagging sound. Fargo released some of the pressure he had been applying to the sergeant's neck. In a hoarse voice, the sergeant shouted "*Alto*" a couple of times. The message settled in along with silence.

Fargo nodded at Hampton and gestured as best he could with the revolver. The lawyer grabbed his papers from Gómez's clutched left hand, then looked to Fargo with an inquisitive expression.

The Trailsman shrugged his answer, then straightened, his pistol still tight on Gómez. The easiest course would be to line up the survivors and shoot them. Or since bullets could be precious in this country, slit their throats and leave them for the buzzards that were even now starting to circle overhead.

As Hampton flanked him, Fargo pushed at Gómez, sat up straight, and got the picture. The sergeant had arrived a few minutes ago with a dozen men, all armed and ready for action. Their arrival hadn't been any surprise. Like everybody traveling in the desert, the soldiers churned up dust.

The Trailsman had spotted that cloud early on today. He'd shifted course, just as an experiment—and the approaching cloud had shifted, too. In this barren land, there wasn't any way to hide from or get around the soldiers. Besides, if they had been of the Juárez faction, instead of the Malgaves persuasion, then there likely wouldn't have been any trouble anyway.

Now Gómez had the Trailsman's pistol at his ear. Only two of his men had died. No, make that three. The wounded man who'd been rolled under his horse was dead. Either that, or he enjoyed staring at the sun with his dull eyes wide open.

There were two gasping survivors with severe wounds. The other seven soldiers, although unscathed, had the look of men who desperately wanted to be somewhere else. Even so, they had to know that Fargo had but one round left in his Colt. If they got serious about continuing this fight, they had a damn good chance of winning.

"Tell your men to drop their weapons, Gómez," Fargo whispered into the sergeant's ear. "Be very persuasive, because my pistol will go off into your head if they do not do this in a slow and friendly way. Tell them no harm will come to them if they obey. *Comprende?*"

Gómez's nodding chin bumped against the Trailsman's forearm, and he issued the order. These men had obviously shot captives in cold blood before, because they looked skeptical about the assurance that they would not be harmed. But Gómez was apparently enough of a leader to get them to start dropping their weapons.

Fargo grunted to Hampton, who pulled Gómez's pistol from its holster and placed it in the Trailsman's left hand while his right still held the nearly empty Colt. This was still going to be tense for a bit.

After an assortment of long rifles, pistols, carbines, knives, sabers, and machetes dropped into the sand, Fargo told Gómez to pass on the order to dismount, hands over head. The cold but wide-eyed stares that came back were further confirmation that the men expected to be shot down on the spot.

Which, Fargo glumly realized, was really the only solution. What else could he do with these men? He wasn't equipped to take them prisoner. There wasn't any jail to haul them to. He had wandered into the middle of a shooting war, and had managed to get crosswise of one faction because the other faction was running the customs station in El Paso del Norte.

Hampton said something about the men being prisoners of war at the moment and therefore entitled to civil treatment. They were standing about fifteen yards away, huddled together where the lawyer's carbine was pointing. Fargo wanted to get some time to think, so he shouted at Carmina, telling her and Day Woman to get out from the middle of the mules and to go scatter the soldiers' horses.

Day Woman gladly complied and even found a long knife and put one wounded horse out of its misery. Carmina was wringing her hands and looking for something to do, so Fargo told her to get his lariat off the Ovaro and loop it around the prisoners.

He told Gómez to pass the word on again that he didn't plan to kill any more folks today, not if he could help it. But still, the incredulous looks persisted. Fargo couldn't really blame the men for not believing them. They'd been on the other side of this often enough to know what was likely to happen.

One beanpole soldier must have decided that he didn't have anything to lose. Besides, he still had a snub-nosed belly gun that materialized in his left hand, moments after his right shot out and grabbed Carmina as she passed.

"I think he wishes to bargain with you, now that we have something for to bargain with," Gómez announced, his voice gaining timbre.

Shit. He could blow Gómez's head all over these sand dunes, and the same thing would happen to Carmina an instant later. Fargo glanced over to Hampton.

"Is this what they mean by a Mexican standoff?" the lawyer wondered aloud, his carbine still at ready.

Fargo couldn't help but chuckle. "Reckon so."

Gómez interrupted their conversation. "You let me go. Raúl lets her go. You go your way. We go ours. It appears most fair to me, *señor*. More than fair, as a point of fact. I have, after all, lost several men, and your party remains whole."

"Our party was traveling through, minding our own business, as legal and proper as we knew how to go," Fargo reminded him. "You're the one that brought on the trouble."

"But you do not understand that Benito Juárez"—he made a spitting effort—"the man you gringos say is our president, is not the president of our nation. Not in my eyes. Not in the eyes of many that he betrays with his stupid dreams about dividing large ranchos among the peons and Indios—"

Hampton started to say something, but Fargo got there first. "Look, Sergeant Gómez, I don't give a plugged nickel one way or the other about politics on the other side of the Río Bravo, let alone here."

"But, *señor*, we do have a political question here. A matter of exchanging hostages, me for that *señorita*. Now how do you wish to do this?"

Fargo glanced over at Hampton and nodded, indicating it was time for him to start talking. If there was anything you could count on lawyers for, it was to delay matters. The Trailsman wanted some delay here, some time, some chance to think without confronting the gritting white-knuckle desperation he could see in Carmina and feel in Gómez.

"You place us at a disadvantage in negotiating this matter," Hampton began, "because if we should release Sergeant Gómez, and even if you should release the *señorita*, then we still have no assurance, other than your word, that you would not again molest and harass our party. As much as I would prefer to believe that you are trustworthy when you give your word, the evidence compels me—indeed, it would compel any prudent man—toward a contrary viewpoint.

"For Sergeant Gómez did give an order for you men to drop all your weapons. Yet obviously, one of you did not. If his words mean so little to you, then what should his word mean to us?"

Hampton was getting wound up now. Although it was doubtful whether any of his audience understood more than a quarter of what he was saying, they gave him their attention. They were caught up in the rhythms and swell of his oratory, the way he was gesturing, carbine in hand. His voice soared and plummeted, rose from whispers to thunders, and dropped back to undertones, moving across baritone octaves like a big pipe organ under the hands of a master.

Even the Trailsman, who didn't much care what Hampton talked about so long as he kept talking, had to work at it to put aside the considerable distraction. Off in the distance, about where the dunes started to the north, another puff of trail dust rose. It wasn't big enough to be yet another band of soldiers. Likely those two boys that were hell-bent on catching up to him. After that lethal run-in with Cimarron Sam, he hadn't had time to tend to them.

Aside from the ominous vultures soaring overhead in lazy loops, there wasn't much else to notice. This was about as empty as land could get. Some of the soldiers' horses that Day Woman had scattered were still in sight.

But the Apache woman was nowhere to be seen, Fargo realized. As Hampton spouted something about the international rules of warfare and the proper treatment and exchange of prisoners of war, Fargo's eyes flitted and searched. Had Day Woman run off?

Couldn't blame her. But Apache were so damn good at hiding that you couldn't be sure, either.

On the dune that rose behind the mass of soldiers, Fargo finally spotted something that looked out of place. It was just a shape, a bulge that shouldn't have been there. While Gómez looked at the orating lawyer and tried to make sense out of the torrent of words, Fargo stared intently at that spot.

He needed a couple of minutes to be sure it was Day Woman. She had burrowed into the sand, with just enough of her head up so that she could see. The little of her that stuck out was coated with dust, so she blended in almost perfectly.

Hampton paused to catch his breath, mop his brow, and swig from his canteen. Then came a soaring paean to the innocence and purity of womanhood in general, and any women here in particular.

If the bullshit had gotten any deeper, Fargo might have been in danger of getting buried. So it was just as well that Day Woman chose then to rise from the sand and cast her make-do Apache war spear: a yard-long saber that she had picked out of the pile of thrown-down weapons.

Gómez started to gasp or shout, an action Fargo discouraged by jamming the man's Adam's apple against his spine. Hampton's eyes caught the motion, but he continued to speechify as the saber sliced through the air. It swept down from Day Woman. The taut arc ended between the shoulder blades of Raúl, the thin man who was holding Carmina by the neck.

His dying reflex was to squeeze the trigger, but he wasn't all that fast. Carmina ducked and lunged forward the instant that he tensed from the saber's impact. His bullet sped off harmlessly, which saved two lives. For if he had hit Carmina, then Gómez would have died moments later.

Raúl fell forward, gasping a pink froth from his punctured lungs. He landed on his belly, saber protruding from his back. Carmina scampered to Hampton's side while his carbine and Fargo's Colt patrolled the rest of the soldiers.

Gómez broke the tense silence with the announcement that it was time for an unconditional surrender. All he asked was that the Trailsman and the attorney be merciful.

11

Today was the Ovaro's day off, which meant riding on a mule with its peculiar government saddle. Fargo wanted to blame the stiff-legged way he felt on that. But he suspected that Day Woman's enthusiasm last night had more to do with his frequent need to dismount, stretch, and walk a ways before returning to the saddle.

They had all stopped this time. The women had sidled off a bit to answer nature's call politely. Fargo wiped sweat off his brow while Hampton refilled several canteens from one of the intestines wrapped around a mule.

"Any idea when we shall come across some decent water?" Hampton wondered as he hung the canteens from saddles after grimacing while he quenched his thirst. "I saw pools near the road yesterday. Wasn't their water potable?"

The Trailsman swigged some of the tepid canteen water before answering. "It's kind of like the old saying that the first gent who ever ate liver must have been damn hungry. That water back there likely won't kill you, but you've got to work up a considerable thirst before you'll want to drink it."

He saw the women returning, and climbed back aboard the mule before continuing. "We can't be more than a few hours out of a little town called Carrizal, and they have decent water there."

Hampton noted that Fargo didn't sound all that excited about the prospect. "Is there some reason you don't want to pass through Carrizal?"

The Trailsman gestured toward Day Woman, who was mounting her mule. "Anytime we travel near people with her along, we can run into trouble. Carrizal has people. It's also got a presidio, or at least it used to." The mules settled into an easy gait across the barren countryside, land not quite as barren as the sand dunes had been, but still mighty bleak.

"A presidio?"

"It's what they call an army outpost or fort," Fargo explained. "The idea was to keep a few soldiers around to protect the citizenry from the Apache and Comanche. Never did much good. They raid anyway, almost in sight of the fort."

Hampton wasn't much given to cursing, but this time he let loose with a thundering "Damn." He even had to catch his breath afterward. "I had hoped that we had seen the last of soldiers after that confrontation back in the sand dunes. Do you think those men will survive, after we left them there afoot?"

Fargo shrugged. "Whether they live is pretty much in their hands now, not mine. But that's behind us. It's what's ahead we need to study on."

"How so?"

"You're the diplomat around here," Fargo bantered. "If the Juárez army has the fort at Carrizal, then all your paperwork ought to slide us through easy. But if the Malgaves faction is running that presidio, we'll either have to fight our way through, or sneak our way around. Thing is, we've got to decide shortly what course to take. If the Juárez folks are in charge, then we can just ride on in. If they ain't, then we'll rein up real soon, before they catch sight of our dust, then hole up till dark. There's enough of a moon so that we can get around Carrizal pretty easy tonight. So what do you think we ought to do?"

The lawyer mulled on that, muttering to himself for a minute or two. "From the way the soldiers we fought with talked, their encampment was to the east of the sand dunes, not to the south. If their army controlled a fort nearby, does it not stand to reason that they would be using it for a base instead of maintaining a field camp? So I suspect that the presidio at Carrizal is not held by the Malgaves forces."

"Then we ought to get through there with some

tedious delay while they check us out," Fargo said hopefully. "A day or two of laying over wouldn't bother me much. In fact, it would suit me fine. I could stand a real bed, even if it's stuffed with cornhusks, and I'd enjoy a few cantina meals if we weren't facing any major trouble."

"I didn't say that," Hampton cautioned. "All I said was that it is very unlikely that the Malgaves faction controls that presidio. But it does not necessarily follow that the Juárez side is in charge."

Fargo sorted out the lawyer's words. "You mean there could be some other outfit, somebody besides Juárez or Malgaves?" He pulled off his hat and fanned his face. "Shit. As confused and quarrelsome as things are around here, that's sure a possibility."

Gideon Hampton agreed, but said his best guess was that any soldiers they might meet near Carrizal would be followers of Benito Juárez, who after all had been duly elected president of Mexico in 1861. Just because things had gone straight to hell in the past two years didn't mean that Juárez was totally out of the picture.

So they rode straight ahead to Carrizal. The twin spires of its cathedral were in sight, rising above an oasis of lush-looking greenery, when the inevitable army patrol appeared. Unlike the last group, though, these men were all in regular uniforms.

Their commander was Capitán Pablo Martínez. He seemed a sensible sort, although Fargo kept his hand close by his revolver throughout the discussion. Martínez first examined the papers.

"All appears to be in order, *señores*," he announced after reading the documents. "So many Yanquis do not respect the laws of our nation. I commend you for abiding by our laws."

It was one of the first times that Fargo had ever heard himself called a law-abiding man, especially on this side of the border, but he didn't see any reason to bring that up now.

"La *señorita,* who has the servant with her, for how long was she a captive?"

Hampton turned to Fargo, who answered, "Four or five years. She kind of lost track of time."

"Madre de Dios," Martínez exclaimed. "That is an eternity." The captain turned to Carmina and spoke for a minute or so, with such speed that Fargo could pick out only a few words.

Something about her father and family and their hacienda, he gathered. He expected it to be bad news, what with all the revolutions and raiding in northern Mexico. But when Martínez finished talking, Carmina's thin-lipped face showed an expression that came closer to a smile than anything Fargo had seen so far.

The Trailsman didn't get a chance to find out what made her look happy, because Martínez had some more questions. He wondered what their party had seen in the hundred miles since El Paso. Hampton did most of the answering with an explanation that they had met a baker's dozen of Malgaves' men in the sand dunes and had been forced to fight their way through.

"I hope you killed them all," Martínez replied excitedly. "They are butchers, killers of children and women."

"I noticed," Fargo interjected. "But we did not wish to be butchers like them, so we left them there without their horses."

"That is too bad. I cannot blame you, though." He relaxed in his ornate saddle. "Let me assure you that your papers should put you in good stead from here southward to Ciudad de Chihuahua, where the legal government of Mexico has not been usurped by such brigands." Then Martínez straightened and hollered something to his men about riding north to do battle with Malgaves. Moments later, they were gone.

Half an hour later, they were at the outskirts of Carrizal. Several small farms, irrigated by a yard-wide ditch of muddy water, flanked the road. Chickens scampered about, dodging the hooves of their mules.

"Hold up," Fargo ordered.

"What's the occasion?" Hampton asked.

"I just figured out how we're going to stay here for a couple days without getting into a fight on account of Day Woman."

"Get her to stay out here?"

"No. Look around. See the womenfolk sitting on porches and working their bean fields?"

Hampton did. "You can certainly tell there is a war going on. Half those women are in mourning."

"Right. In black dresses and veils that cover their faces and most of their hair."

Hampton caught on. They sent Carmina into town. She returned in fifteen minutes with a parcel. She had to explain matters to Day Woman, but when the Apache woman emerged from some bushes, she was attired as a Mexican widow, deep in mourning. She even sobbed whenever anybody said anything to her, so that her speech wouldn't give her away. It wasn't real comfortable, wearing heavy black clothing in this blistering sun, but it had to be more pleasant than getting shot.

Proprietries being what they were in gossip-ridden and religious little towns, Fargo had to share a mud-walled room with Gideon Hampton, who seemed as determined to catch up on resting as Fargo was to catch up on eating and drinking.

During their two-day stay in Carrizal, Fargo spent a lot of time in the cantina. Several times, the Trailsman rode out to examine the countryside to the north. Ample dust rose from the desert, and there was evidence of scattered evening campfires in the distance. But there were pieces of at least two armies fighting out there, as well as vagrant bands of Apache and Comanche. His rides were mostly an effort to stay busy doing something. Fargo felt reasonably certain that if the boys were still following him, they'd show up in Carrizal.

It looked almost certain that they'd got caught up in all that fighting. They didn't appear at the livery stable or the open-air market across the town plaza from the cathedral. They never entered the cantina, either.

Hardly anybody showed up that didn't live in Carrizal. The town had never been big, but it had been much more lively a few years back. The owner, who also tended bar, explained in halting English that there just wasn't much traffic on the road these days. All that fighting to the north understandably discouraged traders from taking their wagon trains down the old route from El Paso del Norte to Ciudad de Chihuahua.

Chihuahua wasn't getting any closer, and their mounts were grained and rested. They started south again.

Two boys were after him, and the more Fargo thought about it, the more it gnawed at him. The boys weren't like Cimarron Sam or the Mexican soldiers. They seemed reluctant to harm the Trailsman's companions. Their feud was with Skye Fargo.

For the first time, Fargo had a chance to reflect on those days when he had drifted between life and death. Lying on the desert floor, he had been stricken so forcefully, so clearly, with the notion that this was hell. Fargo shifted in his saddle to glare back at the little Mexican town they were leaving.

The sun blazed down on the faded adobe hovels. The streets were baked so hard that even the tufted desert grass and cactus had to struggle to survive in the shadows cast by the one-room huts. So many women wore black, the badge of mourning.

The presidio didn't protect against the Apache or Comanche. It merely housed soldiers, and with the crazy wars that were spreading across this bleak land, many of them would soon be dead. Maybe they deserved it, these people who placed more value on a woman's scalp than on her life.

Skye Fargo was not like Gideon Hampton; he had never been a man to change things, to seek the power to change things. The Trailsman accepted what he found and learned to deal with it. He had made a living out of helping other people deal with life's challenges and adversities.

But as he turned back to scan the northern vista, Fargo admitted to himself that there was a chance that the boys, if they were still on his trail, might get lucky. Living the way he did, there was always a chance that a sniper's bullet could take him out. But Fargo wanted to know all about that bullet if one was coming.

Hell, maybe there never was a reason for killing. Only a few days ago, Fargo had killed several alleged soldiers, and he didn't have a damned thing against any one of them personally. But the boys obviously thought they had a reason. Fargo just wished he could figure out what it was. Because sometimes there didn't seem to be any more logic in the real world than there had been in those laudanum-laden dreams.

Just as soon as the town was behind them, Day Woman wanted to change clothes. Fargo passed the word that she shouldn't, not until they had passed the presidio, which was two or three miles south of town.

When they got near it, they met more soldiers—polite and friendly, but still soldiers. Hampton wanted to talk to the commander of the fort. Fargo wanted to press on.

"Colonel López is very close to President Juárez," the lawyer argued. "As you may recall, our President Lincoln would like to assist Benito Juárez in any way possible. I might gather a great deal of useful information if I had the opportunity to talk to Colonel López. I wanted to do so earlier, during our stay in town, but he was away. He just returned last night. Unfortunately, I gather that he will not be free to meet with me until this afternoon."

Keeping his voice to a whisper so that the nearby soldiers wouldn't hear him, Fargo presented his side. "The idea is to get to Chihuahua, which we won't do if we're hanging around an army post. And it's not a safe place for one of us." He flicked his eyes toward Day Woman, who was pouring off sweat, soaking her widow's weeds, whose blackness amplified the potent heat of the blazing sun.

"I concede that," Hampton whispered. "By the way, Fargo, did anyone ever tell you that you might have done pretty well for yourself if you had taken to the bar?"

"I've taken to a lot of bars," the Trailsman commented. "But that's neither here nor there. Point is, you want to stay around this presidio, but she needs to get the hell away. And there's no judge handy to decide who's more right."

Hampton frowned and slumped, then brightened. "I am amenable to a compromise, although I don't have anything in mind."

"How about this? Do you think you can handle ten miles of this on your own?" the Trailsman probed.

"I suppose. There are soldiers all over here, and we and they are on the same side for a change. I should be safe enough."

"Then you can hang around the fort today. We'll go on. I don't want Day Woman around soldiers any more than absolutely necessary."

"Go on where?"

"There are springs about ten miles south. We'll set up camp there. You can meet us there at sundown. That'll give you a chance to talk with Colonel López, and that'll keep Day Woman's hair from getting sold off her head."

Hampton allowed that was fair enough, all the way around, and turned his mule toward the stone-walled presidio.

After all that time in the lawyer's company, traveling in relative silence was something of a novelty for the Trailsman. A welcome one, though. Even Carmina and Day Woman rode silently. They must have pretty well chattered themselves out during their stay in Carrizal.

Just about the time that the Trailsman's growling stomach confirmed the short shadows' announcement that it was noon, they pulled up at a spot called Ojo Caliente. Since *caliente* meant hot, that made sense, because these were hot springs. *Ojo* meant "eye," and Fargo couldn't figure out why that word got applied to hole in the ground.

The place was just as he remembered: a tree-lined rock basin about thirty feet long and fifteen feet wide, generally between three and six feet deep. The water sat at a comfortable temperature. In the whole dusty expanse from Independence, Missouri, to Chihuahua, Mexico, there wasn't a better place to ease a man's trail-sore muscles. All he had to do was keep the horseflesh from beating him to the pool, because four-legged animals liked the warm water just as much as their two-legged masters did.

With gestures that got the message across, he told Day Woman to shuck her widow's gear and get the mules tied down after letting them drink but before they got the notion of wading in.

She gladly doffed her black dress and veil right on the spot. Since she didn't have a stitch on underneath, and because he'd been sleeping by himself for the past couple nights, Fargo forgave himself for staring at her muscled body. If it hadn't been for her missing nose, she'd be a damn attractive woman. Even at that, Fargo didn't much care one way or another about rubbing noses with a gal. Granted, he and Day Woman argued a lot and she liked to tease him about what real men did or didn't. But she seemed to think he was man enough at night, and that was what counted.

Carmina rode up beside him, blocking his view. He had planned to dismount and start pulling off clothes before jumping into the water, but something looked peculiar about her. What? She was smiling, that was what. Carmina never smiled, never showed any emotion, come to think of it. Yet she'd been like this ever since that captain had talked to her.

It was a caution how difficult it was to get himself to strike up a conversation with this woman, even though they had been traveling together for weeks. When she talked, it was with Day Woman. Some nights she slept with Hampton, some nights by herself. Her face had been an impassive mask. Fargo wished he had Hampton's facility for summoning words. Finally he decided the direct approach was best.

"Carmina, back on the other side of Carrizal, we ran across some soldiers. The captain there told you something and you've been looking real pleased ever since."

She smiled higher, and it didn't break her face. "He knows my family, Señor Fargo."

"He had news of your kinfolk?"

"*Sí*. My father and mother, my sisters and little brother, they are all well. My father had to abandon his rancho, which was too far from the town for the soldiers and others to protect from the Indios. But he has land close by the city of Chihuahua, and they are there. The *capitán* says they are well and that they still ask of me."

"I'd be surprised if they didn't," Fargo prodded, dismounting and then offering her a hand.

"It made me feel good inside to know that they still care, even though I was by Indios taken and . . ." She lit on the ground and caught her breath before continuing. "And made, as you know, not a virgin, *señor*. If they knew that of me, they would not still care whether I lived or died."

Fargo's anger welled and he damn near bit off the tip of his own tongue. He took it out on his shirt, almost ripping it open before he wrestled one sleeve off.

"Carmina, dammit, is that your problem? Is that why you never care about anything? Why you're just a bump on the back of a mule? Because you think that you're so disgraced that no one will care about you?"

His words had come in a torrent, too fast for her to grasp at once. She spoke English, but she wasn't all that comfortable with the language.

It could have been just sweat, but moisture was gathering beneath her eyes when she lifted them to meet his. "*Señor,* I am disgraced. The only one who cares about me is my sister."

"Day Woman?"

She nodded and stepped back, giving Fargo room to finish pulling his shirt off.

"Think back for a minute, lady," Fargo growled. "Recall when we ran across that first bunch of soldiers. And they grabbed you for a hostage? If it's so true that nobody cares about you, then why didn't we just leave you in their hands? It would have been a hell of a lot easier, all the way around."

That made her think for a bit. Fargo was now certain that he saw tears starting to trickle down her thin face.

"Perhaps it is as you say, *señor*. But if you care, why do you sleep with my sister, not with me?"

The true answer was awful complicated. Fargo wasn't even sure he could put it into words. The fact was, Day Woman seemed to enjoy what they did in the bedroll. The one time he'd bedded Carmina, she had just gone through the motions, and there wasn't much motion, at that.

Carmina did sleep with Hampton, off and on, likely because she thought that was what she was supposed to do with any men that were in camp. Hampton was too much of a gentleman to complain—and why should he have any complaints? Any woman was better than none at all. But when given a choice, Fargo wanted to take his pleasure with a woman who was taking her pleasure, too.

The Trailsman hated to even guess how many men had had their way with Carmina. She was a hardened woman who had built a thick shell around herself. She had persuaded herself that no one cared about her, and she protected herself by doing her best to make sure she didn't care about anyone or anything. But paradoxically, she was also just a girl of seventeen or eighteen who still stammered and blushed when she had to say "virgin." How in hell was he going to explain all that to her?

"After the first time, I did not approach you again because I did not think you cared for me, and I wanted to respect your feelings," Fargo soothed.

"Why do you say such a thing about me?" Her voice was sharp.

"Because you seemed to have no passion for me." The words were coming more easily to Fargo now that he'd thought about this.

"You are a *cabrón*." She wasn't quite shrieking, but her voice was rising and her eyes were flashing. "You do not give woman a chance, do you?"

"Just how much of a chance do you want, honey?" Fargo undid his belt and dropped his trousers. He started stepping out of his boots. The pool was looking better by the second. "There are a lot of ways to care about somebody, lady, and I did care enough to do as you wanted, to try to get you across a thousand miles of desert to your family."

Fargo thought his words had been temperate. But Carmina must not have agreed, because her hand lashed out with a stinging slap to his cheek. "You pig. You do not care at all."

Truth be told, Fargo's main concern was with getting away from a distraught woman. He'd rather face Comanches any day. The irony of it struck Fargo. She hated herself because she was "disgraced," but she was also angry at him for not furthering her disgrace. That was it. It didn't make a lot of sense, but a woman's feelings seldom did.

He saw another slap coming and reached out, blocking it with his arm as he grasped her shoulder. She twisted. There was a loud rip, and he found himself holding her smock, while Carmina, naked as a jaybird, danced back before darting toward him, her jaw set. "Show me that you care, *señor*. Do not talk like Señor Hampton. Show me."

The Trailsman was beginning to get the idea that Carmina wanted to be wanted. The rising upthrust under his balbriggans told him that he was starting to uphold his end of that proposition. But he sure didn't want to chase her through the thorny brush that grew between the trees beside the pool. So he lunged forward and swept her up, one arm under her shoulders and the other under her thrashing knees. Slowly, he leaned down and kissed her before turning and dropping her into the water.

She splashed enough to get him wet before he joined her, even though he wasted no time in shedding his balbriggans and jumping in.

Ever since he'd first seen this pool, as an apprentice guide and wagonmaster years ago, he'd dreamed of sharing its warm water with a beautiful woman. But in the following years, there never had been a woman with the party. Now he had the chance to make a dream come true.

Carmina looked like a dream, too. A receding one, when he looked up and the spray settled. She floated on her back, drifting away from him. Her pert breasts broke the surface in two smooth and tempting mounds. Her firm thighs were spread just enough so that he could enjoy the view where they joined in a matted and glistening cluster. The only thing that wasn't like his dream was how she was shouting stuff about what a bastard he was for throwing her into the water.

The easiest way to quiet that was to paddle over there, and either hold her head underwater or start kissing her furiously. Fargo took the kinder course. Naturally, he had to make sure she stayed afloat, even though the water wasn't more than a yard deep here, so his hands moved down her back, past the small to the swell of her buttocks, which he pressed against his own throbbing desire.

She met that with her own impatient mound, rubbing it against his shaft. It just might be possible to start in while they were still afloat. But Fargo wasn't certain, and besides, Carmina wanted to know that he wanted her.

He broke off the kiss, even though she was fixing to pull his tongue out by its roots, and nibbled at an earlobe while her hot, panting breath ruffled his whiskers. He pushed his foot toward bottom, found it, and straightened, bringing her up with him.

Carmina was just a slip of a gal anyway, and with the added buoyancy she had in the water, he hoisted her so that her nipples glistened before his eyes. Fargo slowly savored each one as she locked her ankles behind his back and rubbed her cleft against his navel, for lack of something better.

The Trailsman kept rubbing and nuzzling for a bit. They must be putting on quite a show, and for all he knew, Day Woman was sitting on the edge, watching and maybe selling tickets. But he didn't care. All he cared about was how damn good Carmina felt pressed against him and wrapped around him, and there was one part she hadn't surrounded yet.

He eased her down on his shaft, and the biggest smile yet flashed across her face. She shouted something exuberant, and Fargo thrust up while she continue to slide down his pole.

On account of the water, this wasn't exactly thrust and counterthrust. When they met and then backed up for another stroke, she floated up slowly. It wasn't quite like any rhythm the Trailsman knew, but he didn't mind learning. Even though they fluttered a lot, they managed to gain some speed.

He was sure he couldn't get any more of himself in her, but he was wrong. As a shuddering shout passed through her, she used every bit of muscle for leverage to impale herself on Fargo. He responded with an eruption that might have blown her out of the water if she hadn't been clamped on him so tight.

That was just the first round. As Carmina explained during a breathing spell, it meant a lot to her that a man would demonstrate his desire by pursuing her, even just into this pool, instead of just taking her for granted like a blanket.

Maybe that made sense. Fargo wasn't sure. However, he was certain that Carmina enjoyed every remaining minute of their time in the water.

He had no idea what happened between her and Hampton that night, after the attorney found them. Just after it got dark, Day Woman materialized from wherever she had been hiding. With gestures, she made it quite clear to the Trailsman that all he had done with Carmina that afternoon, he could do with her—if he was a real man. Fargo never turned down a challenge like that.

12

South of Ojo Caliente, nothing happened quite the way Skye Fargo had expected. The Trailsman had presumed that the last hundred miles to Carmina's father's estate would be an extended skirmish. But the road had been peaceful, almost serene. No quarrelsome Indians, no rabid soldiers, no corrupt and greedy officials, not even the usual *bandidos* and *ladrones*.

The hacienda of Don Miguel Pedro Gallegos was laid out like a small town. The main house sat on one side of a plaza; it contained a well, a row of beehive-shaped baking ovens, and a pit where men were now laying in a fire to burn down to coals for tonight's celebration in honor of Carmina's return. Several bunk-houses and similar outbuildings flanked the main house. Right across from the main house stretched a long stable.

The main house was stone and adobe, so the inside was tolerably cool, even in the blistering heat of a blazing afternoon.

In the library, Don Miguel poured brandy for himself and his guests, the Trailsman and the attorney, before sitting in a fancy wooden thronelike chair that was covered with tooled leather. "You cannot know what joy you have returned to my life when you returned my precious daughter," he began.

Fargo sipped his peach brandy before answering. "Well, as I'm sure Gideon explained before I got here, I was just doing my duty as a citizen. More than that, it was my duty as a man—after she and Day Woman found me bleeding to death in the desert and tended to me. People help you, you help them. That's the only way any of us get by."

Don Miguel nodded and smiled, his teeth almost glowing in this dark room whose walls were lined with leather-bound books. "In this time of turmoil, you cannot know how pleased I am to meet a man who still believes in the right things and acts upon them."

"Turmoil?" Fargo wondered aloud. "Between the border and Ojo Caliente, we ran across more than our share. But from there to here, this country was more peaceable than I'd ever seen it."

Gideon broke in. "I found out why, Fargo. The French have taken over Chihuahua. Many residents have fled this area, and others are lying low. It was merely our good fortune that we didn't encounter a French patrol—they must have been tied up elsewhere."

"French?" Fargo drained the brandy so it wouldn't slosh when he slammed the glass down. "Let me see if I've got this straight. You've got Benito Juárez and his followers, right?"

"Of which Don Miguel is one," Hampton explained. "And which our government considers to be the legitimate government of Mexico."

Fargo nodded. "Then there was General Malgaves and his crew."

"Foolish reactionists," Don Miguel interjected. "In Mexico, there are people of great wealth like me, but most are of unspeakable poverty. Matters must change, whether I personally wish for them to or not. But Malgaves believes he can keep the old order.

"I support President Juárez because, I believe, under his way the transition would be orderly. If the Malgaves side wins, indeed I might keep my big estate—for a time. Then as certainly as the dawn follows the darkness, there would come an uprising, a brutal and savage revolt, and I would lose my life and my family. Those are what is truly important, Señor Fargo. If you have those, you can find land. If you have not those, then all that land is good for is to bury you under, *sí?*"

That made sense to Fargo, so he went back to what hadn't made sense. "You're right about that, Don Miguel. But didn't I hear you mention that there were French soldiers about? Last time I checked, France was about an ocean away from Mexico. What are they doing here?"

Don Miguel turned to Hampton, who finished lighting a long, slender cigar before explaining.

"To make a long story short, Mexico borrowed a lot of money in Europe to finance new roads, railroads, universities—things that Juárez believed the nation needed. Then Mexico ran into trouble paying off its loans, which were mostly from France, although England and Belgium also lent money here. So France has taken steps to make sure it gets repaid."

"You have to figure that if you borrow money and don't pay it back, the banker's going to do something. But it's kind of funny, though, the idea of repossessing a whole country." Fargo noticed that his host was refilling his brandy, and relaxed with his full glass.

It was Don Miguel who wasn't relaxed. "This is not humorous. When Spain ran Mexico, it tore millions in gold and silver and gems from our soil. Treasure was hauled away by the shipload. They owe us. We do not owe them."

Hampton, ever the diplomat, smoothed that away. "You are indeed right, Don Miguel, in a philosophical and moral sense. But that is not the issue here. What we must realize is that, whether they are right or wrong, the French want to ensure that their loans are repaid. So they landed an army at Vera Cruz some time ago.

"That army has conquered its way northward. Mexico City has fallen to them, and President Juárez has fled. Just last week, the French took over Chihuahua, without firing a shot. Juárez and his people took to the mountains, where they plan to escape northward. They will make a stand somewhere near the border, build their forces, then march south and retake their nation from the French."

It sounded like Hampton had pretty well succeeded in his mission of finding out the situation in Mexico: confusing as hell, with at least two local armies fighting each other when they weren't fighting various Indians or a foreign army.

Fargo absorbed all that. "Then it sounds like our

best course is to get out of here while things are still as quiet as they're likely to be for a spell."

Hampton nodded, but Don Miguel had other notions. "Señor Fargo, do you wish for my daughter's hand in marriage?"

The Trailsman damn near dumped brandy all over himself. Why hadn't Don Miguel just done something simple, like draw a pistol on him? Did Fargo have a chance to hire that smooth-tongued Hampton to figure out an answer to that one? And if Don Miguel was of a mind to force somebody into marrying Carmina just because that somebody had trifled with her, then Hampton ought to be higher on the list than the Trailsman.

"Your daughter is a comely young women," Fargo began. "But I'm not the marrying type. There's some things from my past I've got to take care of before I can ever settle down. I don't want to go into all that." He gave Don Miguel his best tired-man-of-the-world look.

Don Miguel shrugged. "I feared as much. But I saw how Carmina's eyes lit and glowed when she mentioned you, how she became giddy when she looked out this morning and saw you in the courtyard. After all that she has been through, so many young women would despair of life. You inspire her."

Hampton looked a bit crestfallen at that announcement, and Fargo became more thoughtful. What good was it to save folks' lives if they lost any reason to care? But why, dammit, did Carmina have to pick him as the reason?

Don Miguel proceeded. "Even if you do not wish to marry my daughter, I wish very much for you to stay, Señor Fargo. There will be fighting here, and you are a man I want on my side. You might have your own plot of land, your own herds of horses and cattle—much of the state of Chihuahua is barren, but you have seen for yourself that these lands are rich and fertile."

Settle down? In Mexico? Fargo wanted to dismiss the thought instantly, but couldn't. And the more he pondered it while sipping his brandy in silence, the more it started to make some sort of sense.

It could be a rough, hard place, but he knew he had the strength and will to match it. He might build something for himself here, instead of being an eternal drifter who never seemed to accumulate more than a few pieces of gold that got spent in sporadic sprees.

Sure, there was a war going on, but everywhere he'd been lately there were wars going on. Blue-coated soldiers fighting Apache, Comanche, Sioux, Ute, Cheyenne, Arapaho, Bannock, Kiowa, Shoshone, Paiutes, Navaho, Pueblos—when the Pueblos, Navaho, Paiutes, Shoshone, Kiowa, Bannock, Arapaho, Cheyenne, Utes, Sioux, Comanche, and Apache weren't fighting each other. Scalp bounties and brutal atrocities on both sides of the border, on every side of those struggles.

Skye Fargo was a man of the gun who found himself getting goddamn sick of living by the gun. But if you had to fight all the time anyway, why not come up with something to show for it? A piece of land, a future, instead of . . . Instead of what? What in hell did he have now, except for his scalp, his Ovaro, his guns, his possibles, some people scattered around, some who felt grateful for his help and others who carried grudges? That, and some dismal memories that gnawed at him? Maybe it was time to take a stand somewhere, and here was looking about as good as anywhere.

A noise interrupted Fargo's musings. Instantly alert, he brought his head up. Don Miguel and Gideon Hampton interrupted their whispered conversation to glance at him before turning worried looks to the heavy door. Fargo was closer, so he got there first, gun drawn as he pulled it open.

Outside was the maid, standing tearful in a growing pool of blood. It wasn't hers. It was coming from a short man in a baggy cotton outfit that had been white before the hole had appeared in the gasping man's chest.

He was trying to say something, and Fargo bent low. The words came hard, for they were the man's last words, and Fargo couldn't make out most of them, since his Spanish wasn't that good.

Don Miguel didn't get there in time to hear it all before the anguished man died beneath them.

Between him and the Trailsman, though, they pieced together something that didn't sound good.

"There are men with guns riding up on the hacienda," Don Miguel concluded. Fargo didn't think the dead man had cut himself shaving, so he urged Don Miguel to go on. "They have uniforms, and they are shooting at everyone. He was herding cattle about four miles out. They shot him, but he stayed on his horse to race to give us warning."

Don Miguel paused and swallowed hard. "That was most noble of him, but for what? We have no walls here, no way to defend from soldiers."

"Then go out there with a white flag and maybe they'll be nice to you. And maybe they won't," Fargo grunted. Here he'd just been musing about settling down, and an army rides in to steal even his pipe dreams. Well, maybe he wasn't meant to be a farmer, but Fargo was a fighter, and soldiers had been pushing him around since back at Fort Sumner—take the women to Bosque Redondo, your papers are not in order, do things our way or die. Fargo was damned sick of soldiers and damned tired of Hampton's diplomacy. Soldiers weren't going to push him around anymore, at least not until he'd decided whether to ride on or settle down on this godforsaken land.

Don Miguel's plaint interrupted Fargo's growing anger. "Ah, that I could merely ride on like you. But with property comes obligations, responsibilities."

"And one of those obligations is to defend your land and your people," Fargo shot back.

"We've got maybe twenty minutes, since those soldiers likely aren't in a hurry. Get the women and little ones in the big house, it's safest," the Trailsman commanded. "Put some vaqueros in the bunkhouse with every goddamn gun you can find. Hampton and I are heading for the roof of the big house. You join us there if you're of a mind to."

Hampton hadn't exactly volunteered to climb the rose trellis with Fargo. But he was being a good sport about it anyway, even though the roof's tiles had been soaking up sunshine all day. Even now, in the waning afternoon, the roof would almost blister a man's feet through his boots.

Hampton stepped gingerly alongside the Trailsman while they moved to the back wall, which extended a yard above the roof. It was a good two feet thick, so it would provide tolerable cover. Fargo saw the ominous approaching dust, then turned to Hampton, who was shifting from one leg to the other to keep his feet from frying. He had borrowed a spyglass from Don Miguel's study. The lawyer had looked somber when he handed it wordlessly to Fargo.

Fargo saw why when it was his turn. They were soldiers, more than a dozen hard-looking soldiers unlike any he had ever seen—polished stovepipe boots, loose red-and-blue uniforms, flat-topped kepi hats with long visors, all armed with sabers and muskets.

"Those must be the French," Fargo muttered.

"French Foreign Legion," Hampton confirmed. "They're a crack, tough outfit."

Fargo nodded. "I've heard tales." He handed the glass back to Hampton. "You keep an eye on them. I'll see how ready we are."

The Trailsman padded the hundred feet to the front of the big house. The plaza had been cleared; the last women and children were scurrying through the door right beneath him. Out some bunkhouse windows, several grinning vaqueros waved rifles, held in clenched fists, and the meanest-looking of the lot shouted something exuberant about fighting to the last man.

Back at Hampton's side, Fargo saw the Foreign Legion was only about half a mile away now, taking its time through a pasture while longhorns parted to let them through. Since they were closer and there wasn't nearly so much dust, this glance through the spyglass told him more.

The main thing he learned was why the soldiers weren't hurrying. For one thing, they had belied their reputation of giving no quarter, for they had two trussed-up prisoners atop one horse. For another, a team of horses was trailing a small cannon on a wheeled carriage. Given a little time, that four-pounder howitzer could produce substantial holes, even in these thick walls.

Fargo wanted to look some more, but found Don Miguel standing at his side. "It is as you wished, Señor Fargo. Now, what?"

"Since they're soldiers, not bandits, they'll probably want to talk some with you before they start their attack. You know their language?"

Both Hampton and Don Miguel assured him they could speak French, but it was the *hidalgo* who did the talking after the soldiers reined up, four hundred yards away. Their commanding captain used a megaphone to announce that this estate, along with its horses and cattle, were held by traitors and would be confiscated for the good of the Mexican Empire.

"Empire?" Fargo wondered to Hampton, who muttered a translation while they crouched and baked their feet behind the parapet.

"Forgot to mention that. Part of the French plan seems to be to set up an Empire of Mexico, and then bring over some unemployed European duke or prince to run the thing."

Don Miguel shouted back that he was a law-abiding citizen who had come by his land and cattle honestly, and that if they didn't like that, they could start shooting for all he cared.

The verbal exchanges continued for several minutes while the *hidalgo* got offered safety for himself and his family and while he told them they were lying bandits whose word was worthless.

Fargo figured the shooting would start just as soon as the soldiers got the howitzer set up, back there out of convenient rifle range.

He was right. The Foreign Legion may have been up to no good here, but it was a professional outfit. Their captain knew that they were sitting out of range of any rifle that would likely be in front of him. While the cannon pounded at the wall of the main house, his other men would divide and come at the compound from both sides.

Fortunately, aiming a cannon took more work than aiming a rifle. The first ball went low, striking the ground with crater force about ten yards in front of the back wall. When the smoke cleared, all that remained were the cannon crew; the riders had split and were swinging wide to the left and right before converging toward the plaza.

What the Legion captain hadn't thought about was the range of a Sharps in good hands. Ignoring how his feet burned, Fargo hunkered up, carbine at his shoulder.

He hated to shoot men in the back, so he ignored the man working the swab. His first shot tore the head off the soldier working the adjustments at the rear of the howitzer.

A man fetching a cannonball looked up of a sudden. So Fargo's heavy bullet missed his head, but slammed into his chest, rolling him back as he dropped the ball. Finally the swabber turned around, and it was his turn. There was one man left on the gun crew, who was fiddling with a powder keg.

Hampton's gun didn't have the range or power of Fargo's Sharps, but the lawyer was a good shot. Good enough to hit the powder keg, breaking it open as it rolled out of the stunned soldier's grasp. Spilling black powder all the way, it rolled into the lit piece of rope, their match for lighting the cannon, which had fallen to the ground after its holder had been shot.

Seconds later, the cannon's carriage was a bunch of wood and hardware flying in every direction. Some of this shrapnel caught four troopers who had started for the left side, then turned back when they saw their cannon crew was in trouble.

Two of them went down with their horses; the other two, both bleeding but still in the saddle, were fixing to die of a foolish belief. They thought that with their muskets, whose maximum range was about sixty yards, they had a chance against the rifles in the hands of Gideon Hampton and Don Miguel, both excellent shots.

Fargo knew how that would turn out, so he legged it to the front wall, to the right, where he could see how the other squad of soldiers was faring.

Not well. They hadn't really expected the bunk-house to be full of fighting men. And whoever was in charge down there had shown some sense. He'd made the vaqueros hold their fire until the soldiers had come within forty yards, where they had nothing but long grass for cover. When the murderous fusillade roared out of the bunkhouse as Fargo watched, Sharps at his shoulder, three of the soldiers fell, and the other two lost their horses.

That situation appeared in good hands, but Fargo still felt troubled.

Damn. Where was the captain and the man who'd been at his side at first? And where were the two prisoners the French had taken?

He looked toward the rear of the smoke-clouded field of death, ignored the screams of anguished men and horses, and spotted a row of trees. They lined an acequia, an irrigation canal, that passed the rear of the stable. He should have realized before that the water-way was also a stealthy way to approach the plaza.

Fargo couldn't see much more from where he was, so he waved farewell to the other two men on the roof and levered himself down the trellis. Hoping he would arrive in time, he sprinted across the plaza to the stable.

He was as surprised to see people in there as they were to see him. But some women and children had run in there when the alarm had been sounded. Among them was Day Woman. Fargo gestured madly to her, trying to explain that there were more soldiers coming up the ditch, and could she please help him kill the ones in red and blue, but leave the prisoners alone?

She finally nodded, grabbed a pitchfork, and hunkered out a back door with him. They got to the ditch, which was a dozen feet wide and brimming with water. He needed to keep his powder dry, so she was the one who swam to the other side. Moments later, she hadn't gone anywhere, but she had vanished. Fargo knew where she had to be, but he couldn't see her.

Fargo thought he was pretty well covered himself. But it was always hard to guess at what others could see. The two officers must have seen him as soon as he saw them, riding up slow on the far side of the ditch, with tied-up prisoners behind them atop a well-trained horse.

The captain's first bullet tore through the cotton-wood leaves, about an inch from Fargo's face. The Trailsman's snap-shot reply had an excuse for missing, since he was so busy getting himself flattened.

But no matter how flat he got, they knew where he was, and they were cutting loose with everything they could fire—muskets and pistols. Fargo knew he'd never get his Sharps up in time. Just stay low and maybe draw them in closer, to where his Colt would do him some good.

The junior officer got stuck with the job of coming in closer while the captain covered from the rear. He rode toward the ditch warily, guns ready, eyes flicking.

Now. Fargo rolled as bullets flew at him. He came up with his Colt, but he couldn't see a damn thing through reeds and rushes. He'd have to rise, get to his knees anyway, no matter how suicidal it seemed.

A bullet's hot breath singed his shoulder as he snapped off rounds at the first target he saw, the distant captain. Fargo's first shot missed narrowly. His second grazed the captain's arm. He connected better with the third, and either the fourth or fifth round put the captain out of action permanently.

But the lieutenant was still there, almost laughing as he drew up his musket for an easy shot at the Trails-man, exposed and holding an empty revolver. Fargo spun. There had to be a tree, something to keep that bullet away from him.

Ten yards in front of the lieutenant, Day Woman rose like a phantom, pitchfork cocked in her slender but muscular arm. Moments after she released it, the bullet that had been meant for Skye Fargo caught her square in the chest. Fargo got to his cottonwood trunk, Sharps ready, but he didn't need it. With four feet of handle sticking out his belly, and three wicked blood-smeared tines protruding from his back, the surprised and horrified lieutenant was toppling off his horse.

Too angry to care, Fargo pushed himself across the water and got to Day Woman's side. She was still alive, although she wouldn't be for more than a few minutes, and there wasn't a thing on earth he could do to change that.

He knelt next to her and heard her chanting what he recognized as an Apache death song. Her days were done; she had sometimes failed to walk the right path, but she hoped the Great Spirit would understand. He put his arms under her shoulders and knees, cradling her.

Before her eyes began to glaze and her bleeding chest quit heaving, she just glared at him. Not because she was angry that he'd managed to get her killed, but because her people believed that dying was something to be done in solitary dignity. And here he was, holding her and messing that all up. So Fargo compromised and lay her back down for her last three hard breaths. He sat there silent, drained.

Minutes later, horse sounds disturbed him, and he recalled the tied-up prisoners, still about fifty yards away. He swabbed his wet Colt and reloaded it with what he hoped was dry powder before stepping over there.

Up close, and without a lot else on his mind, he recognized them as the two boys who had been following him ever since Persnickety Springs. It was time for a talk. He cut their leg ropes so they could dismount, and sliced their gags.

The taller one spoke first. "It just would turn out that way. We finally get you alone, and them frogs caught us first, so you've got the gun and we don't, you murdersome son of a bitch. Them Frenchies didn't kill us, on account of that they didn't want to piss off the good old United States while they're taking over Mexico, but they might as well have. You're fixing to do it, and you're a mean bastard that'll likely roast us first, the Apache way, or cut us up plenty, like them Comanches do."

"You boys brothers?" the Trailsman asked.

They both nodded, and then the little one spoke. "That's all the family we have since you orphaned us over by Yuma."

"When did all this happen?"

"You oughtta know," the big one spat. "Couple months ago. You and your late partner, you raided our ma and pa's remote little stage station while we was out hunting. We come back to nothing but their bodies and some smoking ruins. Maybe we won't be the ones that makes you pay, mister, but if there's a just God in heaven, somebody will. We done our best."

Fargo's mind raced. "So you followed the raiders' trail east from Yuma to Persnickety Springs, where things got real confused on account of some fractious Apache."

"Wherein your partner must have got hisself killed," the younger boy explained. "But you rid out somehow, tied up with the Mexican lady and that Apache gal—"

"Boys," Fargo interjected, "you can believe me or not, as you're of a mind to, but we're on the same side here. I was looking for those selfsame murdersome men when I rode to Persnickety Springs."

They looked incredulous. It was all starting to fit together. Fargo explained his own life, his own quest for those two men—who had done the same thing, in the same way, to his family. He finally told them how he had taken a new name, Skye Fargo.

"Then you'd be the one they call the Trailsman?" the blond one marveled before starting to sob. "Oh, boy, did we ever screw up. Risking our lives, wasting all that time on a wild-goose chase."

His older brother nodded while his voice caught.

Fargo cut the restraints off their hands. "No, boys, it wasn't a waste. You did what was right. You just got confused by some mighty perplexing sign. Those two bastards are tricky, or I'd have caught up to them long ago."

They nodded, but the older still muttered about wasting all that effort, all that time.

Fargo grabbed his shoulders and shook him, forcing him to meet his level gaze. If he could persuade the boy, he could persuade himself. But the words wouldn't come.

The younger one spoke. "We did the right thing. As much as we could. Maybe it's time for us to get on to something else, being as you're bent on the same errand."

"That's right." Fargo agreed, knowing now that he wasn't ever going to settle down in Mexico. "You can chase after them or not. But I know I have to."

The boys looked relieved. "You're staying after them," the older and darker one whispered. "So we don't have to."

Fargo nodded. "No, you don't have to. There's plenty of other things to do. Why, just a little while ago I got the idea that Don Miguel wouldn't mind having a couple of hard-fighting gringos here to help him fight off the French, the Malgaves faction, the Apache, the Pima. He's got a right pretty daughter, too." Fargo caught his breath. "And whenever the day comes that I catch those bastards that killed your family and mine, I'll make sure you know."

In the last light of day, the older one's eyes lifted toward the festive noises and cooking smells that were emanating from the plaza, over across the ditch and past the stable.

"What's going on over there? Some kind of victory festival?" he asked.

"Now it is," the Trailsman explained, realizing from the sounds that the clash with the French Foreign Legion was over. The foreigners hadn't expected a real fight, and any that were left must have retreated. "It started out as a welcome for Carmina. After five years as a captive, she's back with her family. Maybe that's a celebration that men like us will never have. But we'd be mighty rude, don't you think, if we didn't let them share some of their happiness with us?"

The boys digested that and smiled with agreement. "Then, what?" the older wondered.

"Well, the maid was making eyes at me"—Fargo laughed—"and likely she has friends that're also curious about gringo men. You go on ahead. I'll follow you shortly."

As a violin struck up a festive tune and a concertina joined the melody, the boys started for the plaza. But Skye Fargo turned back to the still body of Day Woman. He had to bury her before someone noticed that she wouldn't be missing her valuable scalp.

Fargo sat for a long time studying her face. She was

truly an ugly woman, with gashes on her cheeks that had been filled with charcoal, so that they had never healed properly. Not to mention the gaping hole that should have been a nose. But Fargo had found a rare kind of beauty in her spirit.

Whether this place he was in was really hell or not, there was a beauty in life. And there had been a fiercely vibrant soul in this woman who had died to save his life. She had been born Apache and she had died Apache, and Fargo was going to bury her with her Apache scalp on her head.

There was killing all around him—killing for money, killing over grudges, killing for countries and land and duty—and Fargo had done his share. But the only killing that made any sense to him at that moment was the killing folks did to protect their own people, the ones they loved.

It was time to fetch a shovel. Fargo straightened and stood over Day Woman. "I guess I'll be moving on soon," he told her. "Because a real man does what he has to do, and he doesn't forget what's become of his people. Because a real man doesn't settle down when it seems easier that way, and he doesn't ever leave his work in the hands of boys. You know something, Day Woman? I'd almost say you were a real man. Except I know the truth. You were a real woman."

LOOKING FORWARD!
The following is the opening section from the next novel in the exciting *Trailsman* series from Signet:

THE TRAILSMAN # 89
TARGET CONESTOGA

*1860, the Wyoming Territory at the foot
of the Wind River Range, where the red man's arrows
made no choice between courage and cowardice,
wise men and fools . . .*

He listened to the sound in the dawn mists, the faint but unmistakable splashing of water. The big man with the lake-blue eyes rose from his bedroll in the thicket of burr oak and pulled on trousers and gun belt. He had taken note of the pond a few dozen yards along the ridge before he'd settled down to sleep, but he'd seen no one near. The faint splashing sounds came again and he began to move forward in a crouch, the morning mists frayed white scarves that lay along the ground. On steps as silent as a bobcat's tread, he pushed his way through the mists that doggedly clung to the land, climbing the gentle slope that rode to the flat ridge. The sound grew stronger, water rippling, being churned, and the pond came into sight as he dropped to one knee.

He peered through the drifting mists at the water and spied the figure that rose up from below the surface. He saw the swimmer's long, thin arms, a shock of black hair that glistened with wetness. He heard the oath fall from his lips as he watched the figure turn and roll with easy grace in the water.

"I'll be goddammed," he muttered as he stared at the girl. She moved higher out of the water as she turned, enough for him to see the curve of lovely white breasts before they vanished into the pond. The big man moved forward again with short, darting steps inside the thick underbrush, and as the girl turned on her back he caught a glimpse of one pink tip that pushed up over the surface of the water.

Skye Fargo moved still closer to the pond as the mists continued to be shredded further by the morning sun. But the dawn mist still clung with enough wispy strength to shroud most of the pond with gray puffballs that rolled like a kind of vaporous tumbleweed. He edged still closer and settled down on one knee in the brush to enjoy the moment of unexpected beauty, even as he wondered where this water nymph had come from in the dawn. The girl turned again, dove under the surface, and he watched her shiny-wet, beautiful little rear rise up for an instant and then disappear. He decided he could move a few steps closer, and he was almost to the edge of the pond when he froze in place. His nostrils flared and drew in the odor of buckskin loincloths rubbed smooth with fish oil and hair slicked down with bear grease. It was a scent that meant only one thing, and the dawn wind blew it to him from north along the broad, tree-covered rise. He drew in another deep breath. The scent was stronger. They were heading toward the pond, and from the slightly musky pervasiveness of it he guessed they weren't more than a hundred yards away.

The girl had surfaced again, thoroughly enjoying herself as she played otter in the pond. When the bucks reached the pond it could well be her last swim, Fargo grimaced. He started to rise, but quickly lowered himself again. The Indians were still a few minutes away, but if she screamed they'd be here instantly and he knew that if he just appeared she could well be startled into a scream. "Shit," he muttered as the odor of buck grew still stronger. He moved to the edge of the bushes, reached down, and picked up a small stone. If he could turn startle into surprise he might avoid a scream. He tossed the stone into the water, where it landed only a few inches from her with a soft plunking sound and the girl turned instantly in the water. He stepped from the brush as she stared at the water for a moment, then turned to frown at the shore.

When she saw him, he was in a crouch, one finger held against his lips in the universal gesture of silence. The stone had alerted her to a surprise and his gesture froze her reaction into a tiny gasp. He saw round, dark blue eyes peering back from under the frown, and she sank under the water at once till only her head showed. He slowly drew the finger from his lips and his voice was filled with whispered urgency.

"Don't make a damn sound," he said. "Swim, underwater, to the other side of the pond, to that willow hanging low over the water." She turned as she treaded water to peer across the pond. "You can come up for air underneath the branches," he said and she turned back to him, starting to open her mouth to answer.

"Now, dammit," he hissed. She caught the urgent command in his voice, drew a deep breath, and disappeared under the surface of the pond. He waited, his eyes on the weeping willow across the water. Finally he saw her head bob up, all but invisible in the small space between the long, low-hanging leaves and the water.

The gray-white mists continued to drift along the surface of the pond, and he suddenly heard the sound of horses moving slowly through the woods. He backed quickly into a thick clump of buttonbush and peered again across the pond to the willow. Unless they made a deliberate search for her, they'd not spot her under the tree with just a casual scan of the pond. Satisfied, he began to move back deeper into the buttonbush when his glance froze at the edge of the pond. *"God-damn,"* he swore as he stared at the small, neat pile of clothes at the edge of the pond: the brown dress, pink bloomers and petticoat atop it, and a towel over all. They see the clothes and then they'd surely scour the pond until they found her.

He cursed again silently as he listened for another moment. Three horses, he guessed, maybe two, he couldn't be certain. They were a damn sight closer now. But he had to try and snatch the clothes away. He rose to a crouch and darted from the brush on long-legged, silent strides. His hand had just closed around the garments when he heard the gutteral grunt of surprise. He didn't turn to look, but flung himself sideways as his ears caught the hiss of an arrow as it was released from its bow. He caught a glimpse of the feathered shaft plunging into the pile of clothes where his hand had been and he kept rolling. He came up on one knee and started to draw the Colt. But he let it drop back into its holster.

He saw three bucks, naked except for loincloths, but there could be others near. If so, shots would sure as hell bring them on the run. He stayed on one knee as he saw one of the attackers, a lance upraised, spur his pony forward. Fargo stayed, counted off split seconds, his eyes measuring distance, speed, angles. The Indian held the lance in his right hand and Fargo, his mouth a thin, tight line, dared to stay motionless another few split seconds. With the short-legged pony almost atop him, he gathered the steel-spring muscles in his legs and leaped to his right. The attacking brave had to make a quick change, crossing his arm in front of him to fling the lance. It was enough to shatter his rhythm and his aim, and the lance went wide, imbedding itself in the soft earth of the shoreline. As the Indian yanked hard on the pony to rein up, Fargo spun and yanked the lance from the earth.

He flung it with all his strength at the man directly in front of him and saw the lance hurtle into the Indian's abdomen. Fargo dropped to all fours and spun as two arrows whistled past his head while his victim pitched forward from his horse, both hands helplessly clutching at the lance that had come out his back.

Fargo half ran, half dived into the pond as another arrow whistled over his head. He went down underwater instantly and swam halfway down along one side of the pond, staying far away from the willow tree. The two braves would be searching the water, waiting for him to surface, and he did so when he was but a few feet from the shoreline halfway down the side of the pond. They spotted him at once and started to race their ponies toward him. But Fargo struck for the shore, pressed feet into soft, muddy earth, and raced out of the water and into the heavy woods. He glanced to his left to see the nearest buck let another arrow fly and then rein his pony up as he leaped to the ground.

Fargo dropped to one knee and yanked the double-edged throwing knife from its calf-holster around his leg. He saw the Indian, an arrow poised on his bowstring, start to move carefully through the woods. The sun had come up to flood the forest with light and Fargo raised his arm, the perfectly balanced, thin blade poised to throw. He stayed motionless, not even drawing a breath, watching the man pass a tree and come into full view. With a snap of his wrist, Fargo flung the blade and saw it slam into the buck's throat just above his collarbone. The Indian staggered in a half circle, the bow and arrow falling from his hands, and he finally collapsed as he futilely pawed at the thin blade that protruded from the base of his throat.

Fargo half rose as the third brave, also on foot now, came toward him, a jagged-edged bone-scraping knife in one hand. The buck, tall with a thin, narrow face and slitted eyes, moved with quick grace through the woods, his long body naked except for a loincloth. He held the bone-scraping knife in his right hand, raised to lash out in any direction. Fargo forced himself to keep from drawing the big Colt at his side as he moved to one side, then the other. But the Indian's long form swayed to match his every move.

Fargo took a hard step forward, darted sideways, and spotted a small glen in the forest. He moved into it, the Indian coming after him on quick, lithe steps. The buck made a feint with the knife and Fargo reacted, pulled away, and felt the blade graze his arm. The indian had plainly planned for his move.

The buck came in again, trying another feint, but this time Fargo only backed away and his foe grunted in disappointment. But he advanced once more, swinging the jagged bone blade in a half circle. Fargo halted suddenly, tried a long left jab, and the Indian swept the blade upward instantly. Fargo felt it graze his forearm as he drew back. But he jabbed again with his left and again the buck swept the blade upward. Fargo feinted a jab and saw the jagged knife start to sweep upward but halt as the Indian pulled back. Fargo's inward smile was a grimace, but he had learned one thing. The brave's reactions could be predicted. To be certain, he danced forward on the balls of his feet and tried a lunge to take hold of the brave's wrist. The buck dropped into a half crouch and lashed out with the knife in a flat arc that made Fargo suck his stomach in as he fell back. He'd tried a different attack and received a different counteraction. He moved backward again, letting the brave come toward him.

His every muscle ready, he lashed out with another jab. The Indian again swept his bone knife upward, but this time Fargo didn't pull the jab back. Instead he dropped his arm, brought it up sharply, his hand closing around the Indian's elbow. He pushed upward, twisted, and the man spun around off balance. Fargo's right came around with all his strength, smashing into the buck's spine. He heard the shattering of bone and the Indian gave a wild cry of pain as he fell forward. He was on his knees on the ground, still groaning in terrible pain as Fargo's kick smashed into the exact same spot in his spine.

With a terrible cry of pain the man pitched forward

and lay facedown in the grass, his body quivering almost convulsively until finally his hands grew stiff, becoming clawlike for an instant before he lay still. Fargo backed away, strode to the nearest still form, and retrieved the thin-bladed throwing knife. Wiping it clean on the grass, he returned it to its calf-holster.

He moved from the foliage to the edge of the pond. The last threads of the dawn mist were drifting away, and he waved to the distant head still under the arch of the willow. He saw the young woman begin to swim toward him, and he dropped to one knee as he waited. She neared, making certain that only her head and shoulders were visible as she halted and treaded water. He frowned at her. "Get the hell out of there before we have more company," he rasped.

"I'm not getting out with you standing there," she said.

"Damn, I'll never understand women," Fargo muttered. "You're more worried over your modesty than your scalp."

"No, I'm just not putting on an exhibition," she said.

"I'll go get my horse. If you're not toweled dry and dressed by the time I get back, I'll help you," Fargo said. He turned on his heel and strode into the woods. He walked back to where he'd bedded down, finished dressing, saddled the Ovaro, and led the horse back to the pond. The girl was dressed in a brown dress fitted at the waist that fell over what seemed a nice shape with very high, very round breasts. He took in the still glistening wet black hair that fell shoulder length, deep blue eyes, a straight nose and well-formed, pale-red lips, a face that held a certain feistiness that added a spirit to what would otherwise have been merely attractive.

"You want to tell me where you came from and why you were paddling around in this pond at dawn?" Fargo asked, disapproval in his voice.

"I came from the wagons camped down below the ridge. I saw this pond yesterday when I rode up this way," she answered. "I woke early and decided to come up for a bath and a swim."

"Don't you know the kind of country this is, honey?" Fargo frowned.

"Of course I know it's wild and dangerous, if that's what you mean," she said.

"That's what I mean," he grunted.

"I didn't think they'd be riding about this early," she said.

"Deer hunting is good in the early dawn," Fargo said. "You've a name?"

"Trudy Deakens," the girl said, and her eyes went to the buck with the lance sticking from him and Fargo saw her shudder. The buck wore a wrist gauntlet and Fargo peered at the markings on it.

"Arapaho," he said. "This is pretty much at the end of Arapaho country. You're lucky. They were probably just a stray band out hunting."

Trudy Deakens returned her gaze to him. "I never heard them," she said.

"Indians don't go around making much noise," Fargo said blandly.

"But you heard them," she said.

"Educated ears," he grunted.

He saw the frost come into her eyes. "You want to tell me how long you were watching before they came?" she queried.

"You mean how much did I see?" He grinned and her frosty silence answered. "Just enough to want to see more," he said and saw the touch of color come into her cheeks.

"I never thought I'd be grateful to a Peeping Tom," Trudy said.

"I guess you'll have to change your mind about Peeping Toms," Fargo commented.

"Hardly," she said frostily. "But I am very grateful," she went on, the ice vanishing from her voice. "My uncle's wagon master of the wagons I'm with. We came up two men short. I'm sure he'd be happy to give you a job riding guard for us," she said.

"Got a job."

"Doing what? Riding the woods?"

"I'm on my way to it," Fargo answered calmly.

A moment of disappointment touched her face. "Well, if you change your mind, I know Uncle will be glad to have you," she said and walked toward a medium brown horse all but hidden in the trees. He watched as she pulled herself onto the horse and sent the animal forward. He immediately noticed the limp in the horse's left leg. "I know," she said, reading his eyes. "He pulled a muscle in his foreshoulder."

"Only thing that'll help that is a long rest," Fargo said.

"I know," Trudy Deakens answered. "I'll give him to somebody with a ranch where he can rest and he'll be good as new. Meanwhile, I'll buy a new mount as soon as I can."

Fargo swung onto the Ovaro and saw the girl take in the beauty of the jet-black fore-and-hind-quarters and the gleaming, white midsection. "That's something special," she said admiringly.

"And not for sale," Fargo returned.

"I'm sure of that," Trudy answered. Fargo pulled in beside her as she started slowly down the slope from the broad ridge. He reined up halfway down where the wagons came into view below. Three old Conestogas he saw and his mouth tightened. Trudy's remark took him by surprise. "You disapprove," she said.

He turned his lake-blue eyes on her. "You're damn sharp." He smiled.

"It was in your face," she said.

"Most wouldn't have picked up on it," Fargo said.

She shrugged away the compliment. "Why?" she asked.

Fargo returned his gaze to the wagons below. "Not small enough and not big enough," he answered and her eyes waited for him to go on. "One wagon might sneak through. A big, strong train would have a chance at defending itself. You're neither. You're three chickens waiting for a hawk to strike."

"We've done quite well so far," she said defensively.

"Luck. And you haven't gone into real mean indian country yet," Fargo said. "You seem to be heading west. That means you're going straight into Cheyenne country, with some Shoshoni, Bannock, and Sioux thrown in."

"We'll be joining up with more wagons in a few days," she said.

"I hope so," he told her, and she gave his handsomely chiseled face a long appraisal.

"Now what are you thinking?" she asked.

"I'm thinking this is no country for greenhorns," he said and saw her dark blue eyes flare.

"What makes you think we're greenhorns?" she frowned.

"Three wagons, paddling in ponds by yourself, two men short," he snapped.

"Then come join us. Uncle Ben will pay real well."

"I told you I have a job waiting."

"I'm not sure I believe that," Trudy Deakens sniffed.

"Believe whatever you like, honey," Fargo tossed back.

"If you think we're greenhorns in danger, it seems to me you'd have a sense of responsibility to help us," she pressed.

"I saved your little ass. That's enough responsibility for me," he returned.

The touch of anger left her face. "Yes, and I'm grateful to you for that," she said. "I've no right asking more of you."

"You've a right to ask and I've a right to say no," he told her, and she accepted his words with a shrug that said she only conceded half of what he'd said. "You'd best see to that horse of yours," he said.

"At the next town, wherever that is," she said.

"Keep going northwest," he told her. "You'll come

to Beaver Falls. You ought to be able to pick up a new mount there."

"I'll tell Uncle Ben," she said. "Is that where you're going?"

He smiled. She was sharp and tenacious and quick. She didn't miss an opportunity and he liked her spirit. "Wasn't planning to," he answered.

"That job will be there if you change your mind," she said.

"I won't be doing that," he smiled.

"No more playing Peeping Tom, either, I trust," she said.

"I didn't say that." Fargo grinned. She allowed a wry smile to touch her nicely shaped lips. He let his eyes take in the very round, very high breasts that pressed the brown dress outward with not even the mark of a tiny point showing, her legs as she sat the saddle outlined against the dress in lovely, long curves. "Good luck, Trudy," Fargo said as he started to turn the Ovaro.

"Wait," she called. "You never told me your name."

"Sir Galahad, Peeping Tom, Passerby, take your pick," he laughed and spurred the pinto up the slope and into the trees. He stopped in the thick foliage and watched Trudy Deakens continue on down the slope to the three wagons. She'd almost been carried off by three Arapaho bucks. Even though he'd saved her, the specter of it would have reduced most women to distraught shock. But she'd taken it in stride. That feistiness he'd seen in her face ran deep. She'd need every bit of toughness she had before her journey was over, he was certain.

He watched her reach the three wagons, dismount, and turn to peer up into the hills where she'd left him. He sent the pinto forward through the hills and knew a furrow had dug into his brow. He wondered why he had the feeling he hadn't seen the last of Trudy Deakens.